Angie: A Prickle Creek Romance

ANNIE SEATON

Home to the Outback: Book 2

This book is a work of fiction. Names, characters, places, and incidents are the product of the author's imagination or are used fictitiously. Any resemblance to actual events, locales, or persons, living or dead, is coincidental.9

Previously Published in the US as Her Outback Surprise (2017)

ISBN 978-1-7638747-1-8

Home to the Outback series
Prickle Creek romances

ANGIE

Prologue

Two years ago
London.

The air was filled with tension, and Liam stood there with his hands shoved in his pockets, looking over her head at the clouds. His lips were set tight, and all Angie could think was that he was keen to see her go so he could get to work for his night shift. The ache that held her by the throat as she fought back tears was almost impossible to bear.

'Looks like more rain is coming.' His voice was soft.

'Yes. It's been a wet autumn.'

'Ange? I'm going to miss you.' Liam reached out, and his fingers caressed her cheek. It took a superhuman effort not to break down and beg him to come home with her.

'Yeah.' She was saved by the headlights of the small black cab reflecting on the puddles of rain as it came around the corner. 'You'll be fine.'

'Will you?'

'Me?' Her voice was hard. 'Of course I will. It's been fun, Liam, but life goes on. We always knew my visa would run out, and I'd have to go back home to Australia.'

She reached down to pick up her suitcase as the cab lurched to a stop with a spray of water arcing through the street lights, but Liam reached out and took her hand before she could grip the handle. His other hand gently held her chin, and she closed her eyes as his lips descended on hers. She bit back the sigh as he kissed her. It was as though he was trying to tell her something as his lips clung to hers. His hand trembled on her back, and she opened her eyes and pulled away to stare at him. His eyes were dark and hooded, but for a moment, Angie could swear she saw a glint of moisture in them, and it almost brought her to tears again. She'd shed many of them as she'd packed. Liam brushed his thumb across her cheek, and she bit her lip.

'It's not going to be the same without you here, Ange.'

Say you've changed your mind. Come home with me. The plea filled her thoughts, but she wouldn't let the words cross her lips. *Please.*

'You ready, luv?' The Cockney voice of the cab driver broke the moment, and Angie bent down to pick up her small suitcase. She'd sent her two large ones to the airport via a courier earlier in the day.

'I am.' She couldn't help herself.

One last kiss. She would allow herself that. From now on, all she'd have to keep her warm at night were memories. Angie stood on her toes and placed her lips against Liam's.

'Goodbye,' she murmured. She didn't look back as she tore herself away and ran down the steps to the cab.

***

The high-pitched chorus of Queen's *'Bohemian Rhapsody'* shattered Liam Smythe's deep sleep. He jerked awake and fumbled for his phone in the dark. He glanced at the bright digital figures of his watch sitting on the bedside table as he lifted the phone to his ear.

What the—three a.m.? And where was he? Another bloody hotel in what town? Liam had to think for a minute before he remembered he was in London. In his own bed in his apartment.

God, he hated calls that came in the middle of the night. Always bad news.

'Liam Smythe.' He cleared his throat, his voice gravelly from the one too many drinks he'd had when the news desk staff had wandered down to the West End after last night's shift. He'd been doing too much of that since Angie had gone back to Australia.

Way too much.

It was time he pulled back a bit on the pub visits every night after the staff put the paper to bed.

'Is that my favourite grandson?' A sweet voice chimed over the line, all the way from Down Under, all the way from the Pilliga Scrub in the Australian outback, to be precise.

Over ten thousand miles away from his safe and quiet apartment on the bank of the Thames River in London.

But Liam wasn't fooled. That sweet little voice belonged to a woman with a backbone of steel. He sat up straighter and ran a hand through his hair as if she could see him.

'Hey, Gran.' He leaned back against the bedhead and reached for a cigarette. Before he remembered he'd given them up last month. 'What's new?'

Chapter One

Ten months later

Liam Smythe sat in the waiting room of the vet surgery at Prickle Creek, a small town in the middle of outback New South Wales. He'd been there for two hours, and his impatience was growing by the minute. Along with the embarrassment that heated his neck every time someone smiled at the cute little dog asleep on his lap—the furthest from a working dog you could imagine—he was losing his cool with the long wait. There was so much work waiting for him back at the farm—since Pop and Gran had headed off on their cruise of the Pacific, and Seb had taken the contract in Europe, Liam had been running the cattle property singlehandedly. He squirmed on the hard plastic chair, and his dusty work boots scuffed the shiny linoleum floor. Every so often, the receptionist would shoot him a glance along with a placating smile, but when he went to the desk to ask how much longer the wait to see the vet would be, the woman would either pick up the phone or disappear out the back. He was the only one waiting now, so surely, he would be next in. In a way, he was sorry he'd said the dog's injury wasn't urgent, but there had been some very sick animals as he'd waited.

God, this is what I get for being a good Samaritan.

A whole bloody wasted afternoon. He was supposed to be moving the cattle from the back paddock to the yards near the hayshed, ready for the truck to take them to the cattle sales in Coonamble tomorrow. He'd have to be up at the crack of dawn to move them if he didn't get out of here soon.

'Oh, Mummy, look. What a cute puppy.'

Great. Just great. Just what he needed to top off an already shitty day. More comments about his cute dog. Every pet owner or cattleman who had passed through the waiting room in the last two hours had commented—some cute, some smart—about his fine-looking working dog pup. In Liam's books, the thing sitting on his lap wasn't a dog. It was a toy. It had no place in his life, in his work ute, or anywhere near a farm. He resisted the eye roll that threatened when the small girl stood in front of him and tickled the puppy's chin.

'Oh, he's so beautiful. What sort is he? We've got a Dalmatian. His name is Brutus.' Liam looked over to the door, where her mother—a slightly built woman—was attempting to wrestle a huge black and white spotted dog into the waiting room.

'Here, you can hold him for me.' He passed the still-sleeping puppy to the child, crossed the room and held open the door for the woman as she dragged the dog inside.

'What's his name?' The little girl's voice followed him.

Liam shrugged. 'I don't know.'

'Why don't you know?'

Another shrug. 'He's not my dog.'

He held the door wide as the woman managed to entice the Dalmatian into the waiting room. He bounded over to Liam, and before she could pull the lead short, the dog's nose dived straight for Liam's crotch.

Can this day get any worse? He stepped back from the cold nose probing his private parts.

'Sorry. And thank you,' the woman said. The door closed behind her, and she dragged the monster dog to the chair on the other side of the waiting room. Liam went back to his chair.

Finally, the receptionist came through the door behind the desk and closed it. 'Hello, Sally. Hi, Lily. Bring Brutus over to the scales, and we'll weigh him, and then you can come into the examination room.'

'But—' Liam bit off the words as the vet nurse looked at him over her square black glasses.

The receptionist nodded at him but wouldn't meet his eye. 'Then it's your turn, Mr Smythe.'

Suitably chastised, Liam leaned back and closed his eyes, thinking about everything he had to get done before dark. Prickle Creek Farm was a good half-hour's drive out of town. If he'd known this visit to offload the damn dog was going to take so long, he would have left the pup in the laundry while he finished his chores. *Who the heck would dump a cute little thing like this in the middle of a dusty outback road anyway?*

And he did admit it was a cute dog. As far as cute went.

The flash of dark brown had caught Liam's eye at lunchtime when his quad bike had rolled over the cattle grate at the edge of the house paddock. He'd picked it up and noticed the pup's back leg was at a funny angle. After two hours of waiting, he now realised he should have rung and made an appointment rather than driving into town to see Rod, the local vet.

A year ago, if anyone in London had told him he'd be sitting here in a small vet practice in the wilds of Australia, nursing a toy dog, he would have laughed at them.

##

Liam mulled over the months that had passed since he'd come back to the farm as the woman, the child, and the bloody great Dalmatian disappeared into the surgery. So much for the quick visit home he'd planned. It had turned into almost ten months. Gran's original request to have each of the four cousins spend three months looking after the farm had been changed every few weeks as life had intruded. Lucy had gone back to Sydney early and then come home and married Garth, who owned the property next to Gran and Pop's. Sebastian had picked up a contract with an Italian magazine that had been too good to let go. Jemima's career was on fire, and there were no catwalks out in the outback.

'I hate to ask you, Liam, but how would you feel about staying out there for a few more months?' The call from Sebastian had come after an email from Liam's journalist friends in London. The work situation over there was dire. Newspapers were cutting staff and amalgamating as the digital readership grew, and the night editions were cut. The newspaper world was changing rapidly and Liam was starting to think maybe a change of direction would be a wise move.

Problem was, he had to find a replacement career. But staying in Australia was enticing, and he'd pretty much decided he'd chase up a job in Sydney when Sebastian and Jemima came back to take over the farm work.

'Not a problem,' he said to his younger cousin. 'Do what you have to do, mate. I'm happy to see the year out. When do you think you'll be back here?'

'Contract winds up at the end of November. So, I should be back in Australia by Christmas.'

'That suits me fine. Jemima is coming back before Christmas. I might even stay out here for a couple more months and chase up a job in the city in the New Year.'

'Are you sure?' Sebastian sounded worried. Liam smiled. He and Sebastian had made their peace in those first couple of weeks last summer when the four cousins had been at the farm together.

'Absolutely. Garth and I have been helping each other out with the cattle.'

'How's Lucy?'

Liam smiled. 'She's huge. It's hard to believe she's still got a couple of months before the baby's due.'

Sebastian laughed. 'It's hard to believe she's going to be a mum. She and Garth didn't muck around starting a family.'

Liam shook his head. 'Reckons she's going to have six kids.'

'Bloody hell, she can have that on her lonesome.' Sebastian's voice was full of disbelief. 'I can't believe she's given up her career in the city and settled in so well to farm life.'

Liam had walked across to the kitchen window and stared out at the golden heads of wheat shimmering in the stiff spring breeze. He had settled onto the cattle property as though he'd never left the outback. The anticipation he felt each morning as he planned the cattle work and the planting of the wheat still surprised him. 'Yep, amazing what changes we can accommodate, isn't it?'

'It is. Thanks, mate. I'll talk to you soon. Say hello to Lucy for me.'

'I will.' Liam laughed. 'And you stay away from those Italian girls. Talk to you before Christmas.'

'Don't worry, I'll be back. I'm looking forward to it.'

Liam pondered the change in direction his life had taken over the past year. The deal had been that the four cousins would take turns to looking after the farm for a year before their grandparents decided what to do with it: sell it or keep it in the family. Pop was getting too old to do the heavy work, and his knees had just about worn out. Liam couldn't believe how quickly he'd taken to the life, and how much he was enjoying the work, but he had to stop playing farmer and get back to his real life sooner rather than later.

Lucy, his cousin, had married Garth, her old flame from next door, and only had a few weeks to go before she produced their first child. Jemima was in New York; the offer of a six-month contract with the Eileen Ford agency had been too good to refuse. Gran and Pop were cruising the world, with Liam settled on the farm, treating this year as a break from his career. Gran and Pop deserved a holiday. They'd worked hard their entire lives, and it was giving him a chance to think about what he wanted to do with his life.

The way Liam felt at the moment, he was more than happy to see the year out. He was doing a damn good job of managing the farm. Yep, he'd give it till Christmas and then consider his options. Then, he'd get back to real work: social issues, tackling big things out in the real world, leaving the Pilliga Scrub far behind him. His holiday here would be over before he could snap his fingers.

He glanced at his watch and looked down at his right thigh, where the pup was sprawled. His leg was getting warm—oh, shit—and wet.

Liam lifted the dog off his lap and stared at the wet patch on his work pants. The little pup yawned and licked his hand.

Chapter Two

Angie Edmonds, new owner and veterinarian at the Prickle Creek Veterinary Surgery, smoothed one hand over the head of the Dalmatian and dug into her lab coat pocket for a liver treat with the other. 'He's going really well, Judy. I can't believe how big he's grown.' She had chatted with Judy and little Lily for longer than she would normally have done as she put off seeing the final patient for the day.

Not that seeing a small spaniel pup made her nervous. On the contrary, the little spaniel was a breed she didn't see out here very often. Two hours earlier, when she'd glanced through the glass panel of the reception area door to see how busy it was in the waiting room, Angie's heart had almost stopped beating. She had jumped back with a gasp, her hand over her mouth. For a moment, she'd thought she was going to pass out as she held her breath in disbelief.

Oh. My. God.

'You okay, Angie?' Cissy, her vet nurse, asked with a frown.

It couldn't be.

'Do you know what he wants? The guy with the dark hair?' Her hand over her mouth muffled her words, and Cissy put down the cloth she was wiping the examination table with.

'The good-looking one? What's the matter? You're as white as a ghost.'

Angie swallowed, and her voice wobbled. 'Yes, the good-looking one.'

'He's got a spaniel with an injured leg.'

'Um, what's his name?'

Please, God, let me be wrong. She leaned against the door with her back pressed against the hard timber. It couldn't be. It must be someone who looked like him. She let out a breath and relaxed. Of course, it was. It was a crazy thought. There's no way Liam Smythe, top London reporter, would be out here in the tiny little town of Prickle Creek with a spaniel on his lap. She chuckled, but her laugh was shaky.

But Cissy's response dashed any last, lingering hope that it wasn't Liam out there waiting to see her. Not a double, not a look-alike, not an image that Angie had conjured up from her overactive imagination. She dreamed about the damned man most nights of the week, and now she'd conjured him up in her waiting room.

'Smythe. Liam Smythe from Prickle Creek Farm.' Cissy frowned at her. 'Are you sure you're okay? You look like you've seen a ghost.'

No! Liam Smythe was in London. He couldn't be here in Prickle Creek. He was not Liam Smythe of Prickle Creek Farm.

But he was. He was sitting out there in the bloody waiting room. Panic, joy, hope, and despair marched through her until Angie couldn't think straight. She took a deep breath and tried to inject some calm into her voice. The way Cissy was looking at her gave her the push she needed to calm down. Cissy would be calling the men in white coats to cart her away if she carried on any longer.

'Yes. Yes, I'm fine,' she said as she leaned over to look through the door again.

That time, her heart had skittered up a dozen extra beats. Her ears buzzed, and her mouth dried.

It was Liam. Just like Cissy had said.

Now, Judy's voice pulled her out of her thoughts. 'Thanks, Angie. We'll see you when Brutus is due for his next vaccination.'

Angie stood back as Judy led the huge dog to the door, closely followed by Lily. 'Give me a call if you have any concerns.'

'We will. Thanks, Angie.'

The door closed behind them, and Angie hurried across to the sink. The moment couldn't be put off any longer. She stared at herself in the small mirror. Her normally fair cheeks held a high flush, and her blue eyes were shadowed. She reached a shaking hand up to her hair and tucked the stray blonde curls behind her ears.

Deep breaths. Total composure.

Deal with this like an adult, not like a moonstruck teenager. She welcomed the anger that was firing in her chest. If she was cross, she could deal with Liam Bloody Smythe firmly and calmly.

The man who had broken her heart when he'd let her leave England without him. The man who wouldn't leave his precious newspaper career and come back to Australia with her.

Translation: he hadn't loved her as much as she'd loved him.

What the hell was Liam doing here in the Pilliga Scrub?

The door opened, and Cissy poked her head around, a frown wrinkling her brow. 'Are you ready for Liam and the pup?'

Angie turned to Cissy with a huge—fake—smile. 'Absolutely, let's get him through quickly and knock off. It's way past time we closed.'

Cissy's eyes were wide as she stepped into the examination room. 'Angie, what's wrong? Are you getting sick? One minute, you're pale, and now your cheeks are really flushed.' The older woman reached over and put her hand on her forehead. 'Have you got a temperature? Maybe you're coming down with the flu? Hopefully not COVID?'

'I'm fine. It's been a long day, and it's really hot in this room. I'll have to take a look at the air conditioner now that the weather's warming up.' Angie injected confidence into her voice. 'Send Mr. Smythe in. Then we can call it a day.'

The look that Cissy flashed her dispelled any notion that she'd convinced the nurse that she was calm. 'Are you going to spill?'

'Okay.' Angie shook her head and sighed. In the two months since Angie had arrived at Prickle Creek, Cissy had welcomed her, shown her around town, as well as being one of the best vet nurses she'd ever worked with. They were beginning to forge a close friendship. 'I know Liam Smythe from way back. It's rattled me a bit to see him out there.'

This time, Cissy's look was one of sympathy. 'Oh, I get it. He's a looker.'

Angie nodded. 'Yep, you got it. But I'll be fine.' She rubbed her hands together and stood straight. 'Send him in, and I'll cope. Let's get this over and done with.'

'I have to,' she muttered beneath her breath after Cissy closed the door quietly. Angie moved to the middle of the room to stand by the stainless-steel examination bench. Her breathing was deep and slow, and she let the anger build. At least she had the advantage of surprise. Well, she hoped she did. She doubted that Liam would have waited out there so long if he'd known she was in the examination room.

No way, she thought. He would probably have run a mile. For the first time, Angie was glad that the signage around the veterinary practice still showed Rod Rogers as the veterinarian. Cissy had ordered the new signs saying Angie Edmonds, Veterinarian Surgeon but they hadn't arrived yet.

The door opened and Angie congratulated herself as she looked up with a professional smile. For a brief moment, she had the advantage of looking at Liam before he saw her. He was struggling to hold the small pup with the shiny brown coat as he muttered under his breath. A grin tugged at her mouth when she noticed the wet patch on the thigh of his work trousers.

When Liam looked up at her, the expression on his face almost made her laugh aloud. It helped calm flow through her veins.

I can do this.

Liam's mouth opened and closed like a goldfish, and his eyes widened. Angie looked down as he almost dropped the puppy onto the examination table. She was careful to avoid brushing his hand when she reached out and moved the small brown dog closer to her.

Finally, she looked up, and her voice was dry and steady. 'Close your mouth, Liam. You look like you're catching flies.' The smile on her face was making her cheeks ache.

'Angie?' His voice came out in a squeak, like a teenage boy with acne. He cleared his throat, and the second time he spoke it, her name came out in the deep tones that had once sent delicious shivers down her back. In the heady days when they'd spent more time in bed together than out of it. In the days when things had been fine, she'd been foolish enough to think it would last forever.

Nothing lasted forever. She'd known that since she was a child, but she'd let herself forget it—time to remind herself.

'Angie?'

'Yes, I'm Angie. That's my name.' Her voice was calm. 'You haven't forgotten me then?'

'Of course, I haven't forgotten you! What the hell are you doing here? You're supposed to be in Melbourne.' Liam ran his hand through his hair, and Angie took a good look at him. His hair had grown, and the slight curls hung over the collar of his khaki work shirt. A work shirt tinged with red dust. She let her gaze travel down past stained—and damp—work trousers and settled on a pair of scuffed Blundstones.

'I'm about to examine your dog. And no, I'm not in Melbourne. What's her name?' Angie leaned down and caressed the ears of the small pup, her professional eye taking in the back leg that the pup was protecting.

'Um, Willow.'

'Not the sort of dog I would have picked for you, Liam. In

fact, I wouldn't have picked any pet for you.' The room was deathly silent for a few minutes until the pup gave a short squeak as Angie probed gently along her leg. 'I'll X-ray it, but I don't think it's broken.'

She sensed rather than saw the moment that Liam regained his composure. He leaned forward, and she stared back. His eyes held hers.

'I asked what the hell are you doing here? Here in Prickle Creek.' His voice was terse.

'I heard your question, and you can see what I am doing. As I told you already, I am examining your dog. That's what vets do.' She spoke slowly as though he were a child. 'You know? You have a sick animal; you bring it to the vet, and we fix it.' This time, she stared at him. 'I'm the vet at Prickle Creek. This is my practice.' Those words gave her great pleasure to say. She stood straighter and held her head high. She'd worked hard to get to this point, and the extra hours of work that had helped her cope with the loneliness when she'd come back to Australia alone had also helped her save enough for a deposit to buy the practice on top of what Mum had left for her.

'But I thought Rod Rogers was the vet here. He has been since he finished uni.' Liam stared back. Angie tried to ignore the pull of the dark green eyes that she'd always thought looked a bit Irish. The whole Liam package had attracted her that first night in the pub at Euston. Funny, the things you remembered at the most stupid moments. The Prince of Wales Feathers pub, that's where she'd met him. The girls had dragged her out on a pub crawl. A hen's night for the receptionist at the practice she'd worked at when she'd first arrived in London. She'd been reluctant to go out, but they'd persuaded her, and said that she had to experience London by night.

Angie could close her eyes and still remember how she'd

compared the small beer garden on the top of the old building in the inner suburbs of London with an Aussie pub—dirty brickwork with exposed electrical connections running above the door. Weatherworn, chipped furniture crammed into the small outdoor space, and a cold London breeze carried in the constant noise of the Friday night traffic. But the atmosphere—warm beer and all— had been great fun, and she'd soon begun to enjoy herself.

And then Angie had looked up to meet cheeky eyes that were blatantly checking her out. Gorgeous deep green eyes surrounded by long lashes, high cheekbones that gave him a fey look, and lips that were too lush for a guy. Lips that drew the eye once you could look away from the depths of his gaze. Jet-black hair and fair skin, Liam was brash, confident, and beautiful. She'd fallen hard. And fast.

Too fast.

And look where that had got her.

'What happened to Rod?' His voice was quiet this time.

'He went to America with his fiancée. I bought his practice.'

'Oh.' He held her gaze with an intense stare. 'I distinctly had the impression you didn't want me calling because you were seeing someone else? So, has your new man moved to Prickle Creek with you?'

Angie waved her hand dismissively. 'I didn't say that.' Hugh, her housemate Jenny's boyfriend, had answered the phone that night, and he'd chatted away with Liam for a while before handing the phone over to Angie. Liam had assumed she was seeing him.

'The message was clear.' Liam frowned.

Angie swallowed. When Liam assumed that she was seeing someone else, she hadn't corrected his assumption. He'd been more interested in telling her about his promotion than listening to her. Angie hadn't wanted him to know how much that had hurt, so she'd ignored his words and let him assume whatever he wanted to, but in a town this size, everyone knew your business. She needed to set him straight, but before she could explain, Cissy poked her head around the door. 'X-ray's ready to go, Angie. I need to get home as soon as I can.'

Angie glanced at her watch. 'I'll come and give you a hand. It will be quicker. It's past closing time. You wait here, Liam. We won't be too long.'

'I'm really pleased things have worked out for you.' He shoved a hand in his pocket and pulled out a set of keys. 'There's no need for me to wait. It's not my dog.'

'Whoa. Hold on there.' Angie took another deep breath and pushed back the unprofessional anger that threatened to bubble out into words she would regret.

Pretend this is anyone but Liam. In fact, it wasn't too hard. The Liam from London had been pale, and his black hair had been cropped short. She narrowed her gaze. He looked like he'd lost weight, too. His face was tanned now—she wouldn't go so far as rugged—but he looked harder, as though he'd polished off the soft edges that too much drinking and smoking had given him.

Usually, when people got her temper up, she would pretend that they were standing in their PJs and that helped her stay calm and professional. That wasn't going to work now. Problem was, Liam didn't wear PJs to bed, and that was a picture she certainly wasn't about to conjure up. That would reduce her to a blubbering mess. Not a good look for the local vet.

'You brought Willow in.' She wasn't going to refer to this sweet little girl pup who was looking up at her with soulful brown eyes as "the dog." 'So, she is your responsibility to take back and to pay the bill.'

'The bill is not an issue. I'm happy to pay. But it's—she's— not my dog.' Liam waved his hand and glanced over as Cissy opened the door and slipped into the room. 'She was left on the road outside the farm, and I knew she was injured, so I brought her in to have her attended to. So . . . I'll just leave her here.'

Angie shook her head, ignoring the mention of the farm. Why Liam was here, and why he was on a farm in the Pilliga Scrub and wearing work clothes was a question she was not going to ask. She didn't want to know anything. She didn't need that angst in her now calm and settled life. 'I'm sorry. That's not how it works.' Her voice was brisk. 'Cissy, we're going to take an X-ray of Willow's leg just as a precaution. Mr Smythe—' she paused as the sounds of Bohemian Rhapsody came from Liam's pocket. He took the phone from his pocket and glanced at the screen with a frown.

'Excuse me, I have to take this.'

Angie spoke quietly to Cissy about setting up the X-ray but couldn't help eavesdropping on Liam's conversation, especially when his voice rose, and he ran his hand through his hair.

'At the hospital? Having the baby?' He was quiet for a minute. 'Shit, Lucy. That's too early. Way too early.'

Curiosity tugged at Angie, but she tried to remain professional. 'As soon as Mr Smythe steps out of the room, I'll hold Willow still, and you take the film.'

'How much? What does that mean?' This time, they couldn't ignore the distress in his voice. 'Ten centimetres? What do you mean you're about to give birth?' His voice rose, and Cissy and Angie exchanged a concerned look.

'I have to go. Lucy's having the baby.' Liam disconnected the call and shoved the phone in his pocket. 'Look, board the dog— Willow or whatever—in your hospital room. I'll come back later and sort the bill.' He pulled out his wallet and took out a hundred-dollar note. 'That's a deposit so that you don't think I'm going to do a runner.'

Angie and Cissy were left holding the puppy as the door slammed behind Liam.

ANGIE

Chapter Three

'All she needs is to keep that leg still and let the tendons heal,' Angie said distractedly.

Jealousy clenched Angie's heart until Cissy placed her hand on her arm after they had sedated Willow and put her in the small cage. At first, her heart almost stopped beating as she imagined Liam with a wife and a child about to be born. Well, maybe not stopped, but it gave a damn good jump.

'It's okay, Angie. Don't worry, Lucy's not that early. I was talking to her in the supermarket yesterday. She said she only had a couple of weeks to go.'

'You know Liam's wife?' Angie forced the words out, as hard as it was to say Liam's wife. That was an honour she had once thought would be reserved for her. It was like tasting sawdust; Liam hadn't loved her enough. What had happened to bring him home to the outback and then find a wife so quickly? He must have fallen head over heels. And not only a wife but a wife who was having a baby. Right now, right this very instant, as the woman who had once loved him stood looking at his cute little dog.

Despair fought with jealousy as Angie realised she couldn't stay in Prickle Creek. Not if Liam was settled here with a wife and child. She'd always had a vivid imagination, and her heart clenched as she imagined Liam nursing a newborn baby with a head full of black hair and green eyes just like his. She frowned; maybe not. Hadn't she read somewhere that all babies were born with blue eyes?

'Lucy's not Liam's wife.'

'*Hmm.*' Angie lifted her head and stared at Cissy. 'What did you say?'

'I said Lucy isn't Liam's wife.'

'Not his wife?' Angie repeated slowly. 'They're not married?' Despair crept away a little bit.

'No, Lucy is Lucy Mackenzie, Liam's cousin. They grew up here together. She's married to Garth.' Cissy laughed.

Angie closed her eyes as sweet relief filled her.

Not Liam.

When she opened her eyes, Cissy was looking at her curiously. 'Lucy and Liam lived out on Prickle Creek Farm for a while at their grandparents' farm, but Garth and Lucy got married last winter, and now the other two cousins are coming home, too. They all left for uni. It was really sad; their mothers were killed in a car accident in Europe, and none of them came home for a long time.'

'Sebastian and Jemima,' Angie said quietly. She should have remembered Lucy was Liam's cousin, but the shock of hearing that phone call and seeing his reaction about a baby being born had put paid to rational thinking for a few minutes and fired her imagination into overdrive.

Liam had often talked about his cousins. He'd told her about his mother and his aunts being killed in a car accident.

But why was he home from London now? Especially after that big promotion he got.

'I knew Liam had cousins, but I'd forgotten.'

'Are you really okay, Angie? You're pale again.' Cissy frowned as she followed Angie back into the front office.

'Yes. I'm fine. It was just a shock seeing Liam out here. Last I heard, he was in London.' This time, she was proud of how steady her voice was, and that seemed to reassure Cissy. 'And I was sure he'd stay there.'

'Liam's been out on the family farm for most of this year. He's been in a couple of times with the farm dogs. Just before Rod left for America.'

Angie shook her head. 'We lost touch when I came back to Australia. I had no idea the family came from out this way. He never said.'

If she'd known, there was no way she would have bought the Prickle Creek practice. In Liam Smythe's hometown. What were the chances of that?

Cissy tidied up the waiting room, and when she left, Angie fed the other animals in the small hospital enclosure out the back. She played with Willow's soft ears until the pup was settled and drifted off to sleep. Then, she slipped off her lab coat, combed her hair, and put on some lipstick.

Despite her intention of avoiding Liam, ten minutes later, she walked along the road towards the Prickle Creek Health Centre. It was mid-spring, and the cool, westerly winds of winter had finally blown themselves out. The sky was deepening to a rich purple-indigo blue, and the small clouds puffing above the western horizon were shot with gold. As the evening star glowed in the early evening sky, Angie closed her eyes and made a wish.

A wish that will never come true.

The hospital car park was almost empty. Two red dust-covered work utes sat side by side near the main office. She pushed open the door of the small building and took a deep breath.

Stupid, that's what I am.

'Hello, Angie.' Jenny Longmore, the front counter receptionist and owner of the cutest ragdoll cat called Sybil, greeted her as she crossed the reception area. 'What can I do for you?'

Angie thought for a moment before she spoke. She'd already seen how gossip travelled in this small town, and she didn't want the fact that she and Liam Smythe had been—had been what? — to get around.

Lovers? Live-ins? Almost engaged?

More like friends with benefits. She was the one who had read too much into their relationship.

More fool me.

'Hi, Helen. Um, I told Cissy I'd get a progress report on Lucy Mackenzie. She couldn't come in, and I said I'd swing by on my way home.' She crossed her fingers behind her back to make up for the little white lie.

Helen's face settled into a sweet expression. 'Why don't you go and see for yourself? Lucy's already back in the ward. Her family's with her.'

'So, no baby today?' God, she felt like she was part of the family with all these personal questions.

'A sweet little boy. Seven pounds! Fastest labour we've had for a long time and a great weight for an early baby.'

'Oh, that's lovely. I'll let Cissy know everything is all right.'

The phone rang, and Helena picked it up. Angie gave her a wave as she turned for the door.

'Angie. Wait!'

She closed her eyes as Liam's voice reached her from the end of the corridor leading to the wards. Reluctantly, she stopped and waited for him to catch up.

'Did you come here to make sure I didn't dump the dog on you?' Liam reached for her arm, but Angie pulled away and headed for the main door. He followed her as she opened the door and stepped out into the car park.

'No. I didn't. I knew you'd come back.' Truth be known, she just couldn't stay away from him, and disgust with her weakness curled in her stomach.

'So, what did you want?' Liam's eyes were shadowed in the dim light. Angie felt for her keys in her deep handbag; it was hard to see in the quickly fading light.

God, I'm losing it.

Her car wasn't there; it was parked in her driveway, where she left it every morning and walked to work. She closed her bag and looked up. The sun had slipped behind the horizon, and the sky was almost dark. A lone white cockatoo flew over, its raucous squawk breaking the silence.

'I wanted to make sure Lucy was okay. And you seemed worried about Willow.'

God, that sounded weak. It would have been the last thing on his mind.

'Worried?' Liam stopped and took her arm gently.

Angie's voice was quiet as she lifted her eyes to those deep green ones that she had once loved so much. 'I came to tell you Willow—the dog—is okay. If you want, you can take her home tonight. I thought it might save you a trip back into town tomorrow. Cissy told me you live out at Prickle Creek at your grandparents' farm.' She said the words as a statement and kept any sign of a question from her tone.

Liam ran his hand through his hair. 'Ange?'

'What?' The diminutive of her name from his lips sent a shaft of longing through her, but Angie pushed it away.

'Look, this is crazy. Let's go and grab a drink or a meal or something. I'm starving.'

'I . . . can't.'

His gaze narrowed. 'Don't tell me your new man expects you to cook his dinner. You never cooked mine for me.'

'Don't, Liam.'

'I'm sorry. Seeing you here has thrown me.'

You and me both, boyo.

But his words, no matter how cutting, had given her a lifeline.

'No, I don't have to cook because'—Angie tried to remember what name she had told Liam, the guy who had answered the phone that night.

Greg? Gavin? Gareth?

Grant? That was it. If she'd known Liam was going to make such a huge assumption, she would have taken the phone from Grant sooner that night.

'Grant doesn't live here. I don't have to cook for anybody. In fact, Grant is not—'

'So come and have dinner with me now. I want to catch up with your news.' His face lit up in that old familiar smile, and Angie knew she was in trouble. Any thought of explaining about not having a new man fled as she stared at Liam.

Deep trouble. Black-haired, green-eyed trouble.

'And I'll show you a picture of my brand-new nephew. I'm sure your Grant won't mind old friends catching up.' Liam's eyes crinkled as he smiled, and she was a goner, back to where she'd been eighteen months ago.

Angie tried to recall the feelings that had held her numb as she'd said goodbye to Liam in their small flat in Notting Hill. Her flight from Heathrow back to Sydney had departed late at night, and she'd insisted that he not take the night off to take her to Heathrow, so they'd said goodbye on the small porch as she'd waited for the taxi to take her to the airport. Two years of living together, sharing their lives, and they had talked about the bloody weather. The ache had deepened. He hadn't loved her, and she had to accept that.

But a girl had her pride. She'd watched her mother beg her father to stay, but it hadn't been pretty. She'd never forgotten it, and that memory helped her stay strong. Then and *now*. Thank goodness she'd never told Liam she was in love with him.

Chapter Four

Liam looked at Angie over the table in the small Chinese restaurant, still finding it hard to believe that she was here with him in Prickle Creek, half an hour away from the farm he'd been living on for the past ten months. She'd lost weight since he'd seen her more than a year and a half ago. Her face was finely boned, yet her high cheekbones were more pronounced than they had been when she'd left. Her blond hair was pulled back in a high ponytail, but the usual stray curls were hanging in tendrils around her face, her almond-shaped blue eyes looking down, not meeting his intent gaze. There was a fragility about her, and it brought out the protective streak in him.

God, she was so beautiful. Another good thing he'd blown in his life. He'd let her go. He should have come home with her when her visa had expired. Now, it was too late. She'd met someone else.

Angie's face had always had a gentleness that reflected the person she was. The minute he had seen her, he had fallen hard.

Love at first sight? The logical, rational part of him didn't believe in that. Hell, he hadn't really believed in love, let alone at first sight. But he and Angie had had something good going— bloody good—and if it hadn't been for her visa running out, they would probably still be together. Call it love; call it what you like. It had been special, and it had ached like a damn sore tooth when she'd left.

He pushed away the niggling thought that told him if he'd been willing to leave London when Angie had, they would have had a chance. They could have been together, still a couple.

But no. He'd wanted to be the big famous Australian journalist in London. It was too late now. She'd moved on already. Of course, she had; a beautiful woman like Angie attracted attention wherever she went. He just hoped that this new guy was good enough for her and that he was looking after her.

Better than I ever did.

'So…' He picked up the fork and twirled it in his fingers as they waited for their meals to come to the table. 'Tell me about the past year or so. We did lose touch quickly, didn't we?'

'Not really. We didn't lose it. There was no point in staying in touch. Our lives have simply gone in different directions.' Angie stared at him across the table, and he ignored the warmth that settled in his chest. She'd always done it to him. He'd been a hard bastard; he should have insisted on taking her to the airport for her flight home, but deep down, he'd known he wouldn't have been able to let her leave when it came to the crunch. Instead of going to work that night, he'd gone out and gotten rip-roaring drunk.

'So, how do you like living in my old hometown?'

'It's fine.'

Heck, he'd interviewed unwilling politicians for news articles, but this was like pulling teeth.

'Why Prickle Creek?' Liam knew he'd never mentioned to Angie where he'd grown up. The country background of the Pilliga Scrub had been a bit of an embarrassment to an up-and-coming international journalist. He'd always told everyone he was from Sydney. *Bloody fool snobbery.*

'I went to uni with Rod in Melbourne, and when he decided to move to the States, he called me to let me know the practice was for sale. He knew I was back in Australia. And here I am.'

'Yes,' he said slowly. 'Here you are. Here we are.'

'So why are you here, Liam?' Angie looked over his head and didn't meet his eye. Her mouth was set in a straight line, and her voice was disinterested. He knew her well, and she looked bored.

Maybe she felt awkward about being out with him in public.

Liam shook his head slightly. Not that it was terribly public. A typical night in the dead hub of Prickle Creek. They were the only customers in the Chinese restaurant, and the main street was deserted when he waited outside the restaurant for her. Angie had insisted on walking from the hospital, which was only a few hundred yards up the road. Apparently, her car was still at her house. The beauty of Prickle Creek. Two cross streets and you could go anywhere without a car.

'My grandmother called us all home a few months back.'

'And you jumped to *her* bidding?'

'Yes, I did.' It was easy to understand why her tone was terse. Angie had been disappointed when he had decided to stay in London when she came back to Australia. She hadn't tried to talk him into coming home with her, and at the time, although he'd appreciated it, he had wondered if maybe Angie hadn't really wanted him to go home with her. His job was more important, and it gave him some great experience with the new technology in the world of newspapers.

'And you've obviously stayed.'

'Yes. But it's only for a short while longer; I'll be going back to Sydney before Christmas.'

'Sydney? Why not back to London?' Is that relief in her voice?

'I've got a contact at the ABC TV network. My London experience should secure me a job either at the studio or in radio.' He had his hopes pinned on this job coming through. He had a good chance, and it was coming online about the time his stint at the farm would be finished, and he'd be able to get back to his real career.

'That will be nice for you.' Angie sounded bored stiff, and Liam's temper started to fire. They'd been close once; surely, she could at least pretend to be interested in his career now. Hell, he wanted to know all about hers. If he was honest, he'd admit to himself that she'd been in his thoughts constantly since he'd come back home. No, scrap that, since the day she'd left him.

If it hadn't been for him knowing she had a new love interest, he might have contacted her as soon as he'd arrived back in Australia. He'd considered it, but he'd always hesitated. It was better to end ties completely. There would have been no point resuming their relationship because once he left the farm, he'd be working in the city again, and Angie's job was country-based.

'I'm sorry if I'm boring you.'

'You're not.'

'Well, it sure sounds like it.'

'Still need to be the centre of attention, Liam?' This time, her voice was cruel, but he knew he deserved everything Angie dished out.

He reached over the table, took her hand, and flinched when she jumped. 'I'm sorry, Ange.'

'What for?' This time, she looked up and held his gaze.

'For letting you go like I did.'

'No need to lay it on.'

'I'm not. I mean it. I could have looked after you better those last few months.'

'Yes, you were a right proper arse.'

And he had been. When Angie had announced she had to go back to Melbourne, he'd tried to put some distance between them and had spent more time at the local pub after work. He had tried to get used to being without her. He hadn't known how he was going to cope without her in his life.

'Well, you always did tell it like it was.' Finally, that elicited a slight lift of her lips. Not quite a smile, but close. 'So tell me about you. Do you live in town? Has Grant moved here too?'

'No, he doesn't live here'

'What does he do?' Liam wondered why she hesitated, and he kept his eyes on her pretty mouth.

'No. Grant's an engineer. He works on the oil rigs. Fly-in, fly-out. You know?'

'No. I don't know much about how it works. All that fly-in stuff happened here while I was in the UK. All I know is about the oil rigs in the North Sea. They fly across in helicopters. How often does he come home?'

'Um. Home for Grant is Melbourne. I believe the oil rig's an isolated site, and he flies there and stays there for two weeks, then flies back home.' For Angie, the gaze she bestowed on him was harder than usual.

'So, does he come to Prickle Creek?' A little morsel of hope fed Liam's curiosity.

'No. Um . . . he's . . . not around much.'

Angie visibly relaxed as the young Chinese waitress carried two sizzling plates over to the table. 'Hello, Lin. How's that bird of yours?'

'Oh, Angie. He's much better. I've been looking after him just like you told me.'

Liam sat back as the young girl gave Angie a detailed explanation of what she had been doing for the pet over the past couple of weeks. Surreptitiously, he glanced down at his watch as the waitress went back to the kitchen. When he looked up, Angie raised her eyebrows at him. He knew exactly what she was thinking; he'd always read her well. Funny though, when she'd been talking about her partner, her face had been set, and he'd found it hard to see past the closed expression.

'In a hurry, Liam?'

'Yes, I only planned on being in town for a short while but the wait at the surgery was a lot longer than I thought it would be.'

'You should have rung and made an appointment. You

wouldn't have had to wait then.'

'I didn't think you would be busy.' Liam shook his head. 'Anyway, it's too late to do anything at the farm now.'

The silence as they ate their meal was far from comfortable.

Liam looked around. The décor of Billy Kee's restaurant was hideous but typical of the Chinese restaurants that dotted country towns in the Outback.

Seventies food, seventies décor.

The once bright red walls, painted to match the long red tassels hanging from the square black plastic light shades, had long since faded to pink. In the end, Liam couldn't stand the cold silence, so he pulled his phone out and scrolled to the photos.

'I promised to show you my new nephew.'

'Are they both well?' She leaned towards him.

Finally, a glimmer of interest.

'Yes, and he is a little beauty. Looks just like Lucy. It's a shame Gran and Pop are in New Zealand. They'd planned to be home before the baby was born. But I'm sure they'll fly in when they hear they have a great-grandchild.'

Angie bit her lip. 'It sounds like you've fit right into the family scene out here.'

'I have.' Liam lowered his voice. 'It's been good for me, Angie. And I want you to know—'

Angie shook her head. 'No. Leave it there, Liam. It's time I was going. I have a few patients in overnight and some medication to dole out before I go home.' She sat up straight. 'What are you going to do about Willow? She's right to go home as long as you keep her confined.'

'She's not my dog. Can't you keep her there?' Liam frowned.

'No, I can't. If I kept every stray or abandoned dog—or cat— I would have a menagerie, and I would have to work twenty-four-seven.'

'Okay,' he said slowly. 'What would you suggest?'

'Take her home, and I'll ask around. It shouldn't be too hard. These spaniels are quite rare and not really seen much outside their native region.'

'Where's that?' Maybe he could take the damn dog back to wherever it came from.

Angie's laugh was light but genuine. 'South Carolina in North America.'

'Oh.'

'Look, I'll find some breeders for you. Maybe we can track her down. She might have run away and got hit by a car and then limped along to your place.'

Liam shook his head. 'I doubt it. Our farm is a couple of kilometres off the main road, and I know all the neighbours. They only have working dogs.'

'Give me your number, and I'll call you.' Her mouth firmed when he smiled. 'But I'll only call if I find anything out.'

'All right. I'm going to be busy anyway. I've got a heap of work on tomorrow, seeing this afternoon was wasted.'

He didn't get the cold reaction he expected. Her smile was wide, and her eyes lit up. 'It wasn't wasted. You looked after an injured animal. And your new nephew made an entrance.'

Bloody hell. She blew hot and cold; he didn't know where he stood with her. Liam pushed his chair back and reached for the bill folder in the centre of the table. 'I'll take her home then. I'll meet you at the surgery after I pay the bill. Or do you want a lift?'

Angie shook her head and dropped her gaze. 'I'll walk.' She dug into her bag and held out a twenty-dollar note. 'There's the money for my meal.'

'No, it's fine.'

'I insist.' Angie put the note on the table and stood. Liam watched as she walked to the door, her back ramrod straight.

Liam rolled his eyes as the whimpering from the kitchen woke him up for what seemed like the hundredth time. He rolled over and looked at the glowing green numbers on the digital clock. Three o' bloody clock. He pushed the sheet back and climbed out of bed. He'd left his jocks on the last time he'd got up about half an hour ago. He padded quietly into the kitchen and walked across to the basket he'd put near the laundry door. Willow—they'd gotten to know each other pretty well over the past few hours—was sitting up in the basket Liam had retrieved from the hay shed. Her eyes were wide, and she whimpered as he looked down at her. His heart softened.

'Come on.' He reached down and scooped her up into the crook of his elbow, taking care not to hurt the leg that Angie had splinted and bandaged. 'This is the only way either of us is going to get to sleep.' He carried the small pup into the bedroom and sat on the side of the bed, rubbing her soft, silky ears. She snuggled into his side, and her eyes closed. Liam lay down carefully and placed Willow on his chest.

Before he drifted off to sleep, he smiled.

Liam Smythe, cutting political commentator nursing a pup to sleep.

He was getting soft.

Chapter Five

'Liam. I need you.'

'What now, Lucy?' Liam ran his hand through his longish hair as he held the phone to his ear. He hadn't even had time for a haircut these past few months. When he'd had a quick shave that morning, he'd been tempted to grab a rubber band and tie his hair back from his face. It got in his eyes when he was out on horseback.

'I need you to come to town. Please.'

'God, Luce, I've been into Prickle Creek every day this week. The work is piling up here.'

'I'll get Garth to come over and give you a hand over the weekend. Would that help?' Her voice was wheedling, and Liam laughed.

'You know it will, you witch. What do you need me to come to town for?'

'A couple of things. Garth's gone to the airport at Narrabri to pick up his parents, and they won't let me out of hospital yet.'

His head jerked up. 'Why, is there something wrong?'

'No. Everything's good, but they're really old-fashioned out here. Mums aren't allowed to leave the babies alone until the last night. Demand feeding and all that. And then on the last night, the nurses babysit so the partners can take the new mothers out for dinner before they go home.'

'Where to? The rissole or the Chinese?'

'The rissole?'

'The RSL club.'

Lucy's laugh cheered him up. 'You are turning into a country boy. And yes, that's our choice out here in the boondocks.'

'The RSL club was the rissole when I was a kid, and it still is.' Liam looked down as Willow crawled out of the basket and flopped onto his bare foot.

'One more thing, I need you to bring something in with you.' He knew Lucy well and knew she was up to something by the innocent tone in her voice.

'What?'

'In the bottom drawer of Gran's kitchen, there's an old exercise book. It's green and it's got a picture of a cake on the front. Can you bring that to me please?'

'No problem. Okay, I've just got a couple of chores to do here, and I'll be in. Anything else you need?'

'I'll tell you when you get here.'

'Hmm. See you soon.' Liam hung up the call, bent down, lifted Willow, and walked back into the kitchen. He'd been out of sorts for the three days since he'd brought Willow home, and there'd been no call from Angie. The pup had been everywhere with him since they'd been at home. He'd soon learned that she was happy as long as she was in his company. However, after that first night, he'd drawn the line at her sleeping in his bed. She'd settled a bit now and was quite happy in her basket as long as he patted her to sleep before he went to bed.

'Sorry, Willow. You have to stay home. I can't see them letting you into the maternity ward.' He put her back in her basket in the laundry and ignored her loud howl as he headed out to his ute.

On the way to town, Liam stopped on the side of the Pilliga Way, where a couple of his neighbours were putting up a big sign on the back of an old truck in a paddock. Well, adjoining property owners. Calling them neighbours was a bit of a stretch. Jim Ison lived ten kilometres away from Prickle Creek Farm on the way to town. He waved to Liam as he climbed out of the ute parked in the red dust on the side of the road.

The sign read: **No Gas. Protect Our Water.**

As Liam walked over, a second sign was raised.

'Gidday, Jim. What's all this about?' Liam tipped his Akubra hat back and read the second sign that was being put up by two of Jim's stockmen. He nodded to them.

Great Artesian Basin. Treasure of Our Nation.

Jim walked over to him and shook his hand. 'Pleased to see you, Liam. You're a hard man to catch.' Jim grinned and wiped his hands on the side of his moleskin trousers. 'But then I suppose running a place the size of Prickle Creek Farm single-handedly keeps you busy.'

'You can say that again.' Liam squinted against the bright morning sun as it flashed on the side of the sign.

'We want to enlist your help. Harry told us about your journalism background before you arrived here to take over the farm.'

'What's happening?' Liam squinted up at the sign that was now secured to the front end of the truck in pride of place for any passing traffic to read.

'Have you heard anything about the Narrabri Gas Project?'

'No, I haven't.'

Jim frowned. 'It's been kept very quiet as the company owners try to get it approved. We suspect there are all sorts of underhand kickbacks and payments being made, so we've formed an alliance to fight it. We'd love you to come on board. We could do with someone good with words. Someone who can put a good report together.'

'Tell me more about it.'

'They plan to drill more than eight hundred coal seam gas wells through the Pilliga forest, and you may not know, but this forest is the largest inland forest left in Eastern Australia.'

Liam's interest flared. He'd reported on a similar issue in the UK just before he'd left.

'The preliminary work has already caused a dozen pollution scares. Groundwater contamination, waste spills, and ongoing leaks from the evaporation ponds.' Jim shook his head. 'You can imagine the impact that's going to have on our properties and, in the long term, on the economy of the local region.'

'I would assume there has been an environmental impact statement?'

'Yes, and of course, they say the risks are minimal and manageable.' Jim huffed. 'So what do you say? Can we ask you to join us?'

'I'm in. I'd be happy to help out, and I've got plenty of media contacts I can get information from.'

'Fabulous.' Jim held out his hand again. 'There's a meeting of the committee after the community meeting next Monday night. You've made my day, Liam.'

Liam was thoughtful as he drove into town. Being involved with a political issue and helping to save the local environment was something right up his alley. The work on the property had been good. He'd enjoyed most of the time out here, but it had been lonely since Lucy had married and Gran and Pop had headed off on their travels. He was used to being challenged by more than cattle weights and crop rotations. Being involved with the alliance would fill the emptiness that sometimes dogged him.

Town was busy, and Liam avoided turning up the street that would take him past the vet surgery. He didn't need to see Angie. He'd tried to put her out of his thoughts for the past few days.

With not much luck.

He called into the produce store and loaded a couple of salt blocks onto the back of the ute, as well as four bags of *UltraGrow.*

There were a couple of calves in the house paddock that he was hand-feeding. It still amazed Liam that out here in the country, you could leave your car unlocked, with produce on the tray of the truck, and it would still be there untouched when you came out.

London had been an eye-opener and had destroyed his belief in honesty. He much preferred the freedom and the integrity of people out here in the outback.

He smiled. Or in the boondocks, as Lucy called it. If he was honest, he liked living out here a lot more than he'd expected.

Liam drove to the hospital and parked in the car park. He grabbed the green recipe book off the passenger seat before he got out of the ute. Jenny waved him a greeting as she spoke on the phone, and Harvey, the wardsman he'd gone to high school with, stopped him for a chat as he mopped the entry foyer.

Lucy was sitting up in bed, holding his baby nephew in her arms. Liam stood in the doorway and watched her as she ran her fingers over the baby's downy blond hair and down his face. It was almost like intruding on a personal moment; the look of love on Lucy's face brought a tear to his eye.

Almost.

He cleared his throat, and Lucy looked up with a smile.

'Can I come in? You're not about to feed him or change him, or anything, are you?'

'No. James Ross Paul Mackenzie is about to go down for a long sleep.'

Liam smiled. 'He has a name.'

'He does. Ross after Garth's dad, and Paul after my dad.' Lucy's smile was wide, and Liam thought she looked happy and content.

'Your dad would have loved that. Being a mum suits you, Luce.'

'He would have. And yes, I'm happy. Even though this little

man came early. Here, take him while I get out of bed so I can put him in the bassinet.'

'So he's okay? He didn't have to go in one of those cribs or something?'

A slight flush tinged Lucy's cheekbones. 'The doctor thinks we had the dates wrong. I was further along than we thought. We can go home soon.'

Liam put the recipe book on the end of the bed and held his arms out reluctantly as Lucy handed the small, warm bundle over. He held the baby gingerly, but after a few seconds, he realised it wasn't that hard.

'It's easier than holding Willow,' he said as Lucy walked around the end of the bed.

'Who's Willow?'

'My new pup.' Liam screwed up his nose as an unfamiliar sweet aroma came from the baby as he squirmed in his arms. 'What's that smell?'

'Poop,' Lucy said with a laugh and took James from him.

'Ew, I'm out of here while you do that.' Liam made for the door.

'Stay there. I'll talk to you while I change him. Like I said on the phone, I have a couple of favours to ask.'

Liam moved away to the open window for some fresh air and looked outside as Lucy quickly changed the baby. After James was changed, she put him in the bassinet and pulled over a plastic chair to sit by the window.

'Grab the recipe book. And bring over a chair. Oh, and in the cupboard there's a notebook and a pen. You'll need that to make the list.'

'What list?'

'I need you to go shopping for me. I was on the way to town to do a big shop when I went into labour, and Garth's gone to

Narrabri. It'll be too late when he comes back with his parents.'

'Okay, I can handle that.' Liam looked down at the recipe book as she opened it and took a laminated page from inside the back cover. 'What's the recipe book got to do with it?'

Lucy smiled at him. That angelic smile that he knew meant she was up to something he wouldn't like.

'Lucy?' He pursed his lips and folded his arms. 'Okay, hit me with whatever the next favour is.'

'One of the things I had to do in town was get the ingredients for Gran's special cake.'

'Yes?'

'And then I was going to bake it yesterday because we only have till Saturday to get it in. The timing sucks.'

Liam shook his head. 'You've lost me. Get what in where?'

'The cake. To the show.'

'Ah, the agricultural show, I forgot that was the weekend after next.' Gran's chocolate cake was a family tradition. Not only did she make it for the family, but apparently, the cake had taken the blue ribbon for best cake at the show for the past fifty years.

'Okay, I can buy the ingredients.'

Lucy's smile was even sweeter. 'I won't be able to make it.'

'So why do you need the ingredients? Looks like it won't be entered this year.'

'Because I promised Gran when she called that you would make it. She was so upset that it wouldn't be entered this year that I told a little white lie. I told her you'd agreed to make it.'

'What?' Liam spluttered. 'Me?'

'Yes, you. She was so happy.'

'Luce, I didn't say I would. I haven't got the first idea about baking a cake.'

'She was crying until I said you'd promised.'

'She was probably crying because you just told her she was a great-granny. I don't believe you did that. Jeez, Luce!'

'Look, it's really easy. Open up to the last page.'

Liam did as instructed, still shaking his head. This family was going to be the end of him.

Puppies, babies, cakes? What was going to hit him next?

'Now you have to listen very carefully. Gran has a secret ingredient.' Lucy took the book from him and pulled out a laminated recipe. 'That's how she's taken out the prize for a record-breaking run. This is the recipe you have to hand in with the cake. And the one in the back of the book has the secret ingredient added in.'

'Okay. Hit me with it.' Liam sat back and folded his arms.

'Oh, you good man. That means you'll do it?'

'I'll be on the phone with you for step-by-step instructions.' He couldn't help the grin that crossed his face. 'I have one condition, though. It gets entered under your name.'

Lucy nodded.

'I've done a lot of things in the past few months that I didn't ever expect to. But diddling a cake-judging committee with secret ingredients? I can see a newspaper story in this.'

'You wouldn't! Gran would be horrified.'

'I'm teasing you. Okay. I can do this. After all, how hard is baking a cake?'

Lucy giggled. 'A piece of cake!'

Chapter Six

Liam stood back and surveyed the mess around him. The light-coloured bench tops were covered with chocolate-coloured goop. Eggshells filled the sink. It had taken about six goes before he'd managed to separate the yolks from the whites. The oven was on, at full heat, warming the kitchen, but as yet, there was no cake cooking in it.

He'd done the grocery shopping for Lucy, dropped it off at the Mackenzie farm, said hi to Garth's parents, hand-fed the calves, moved the irrigation sprinkler, herded a mob of cattle from the front paddock to the side paddock, and then had come back inside to bake this cake.

How hard could it be? Really? All he wanted to do was put his feet up and have a cold beer.

The reality was very different, especially when Lucy wasn't answering her phone for the numerous questions he had. He'd gathered the ingredients—finding them in Gran's neatly labelled containers in the walk-in pantry wasn't a problem—but when the recipe talked about weights, Liam had no idea how to figure that out. A deep search of the pantry finally unearthed a pair of food scales.

Half an hour later, despite the state of the kitchen, he was feeling mellow—thanks to the occasional slug of Gran's secret ingredient.

'That's a good girl,' he muttered as he searched in the cupboards for a sandwich cake tin. Willow was licking the spilled egg yolks from the once-clean floor.

What the hell is a sandwich tin?

He gave up looking and picked up the bottle of the secret

ingredient. He took another slurp; it was hygienic; he'd already measured out the cup of whisky that replaced the milk in the recipe, plus a spare cup in case the first mix failed. The bottle was now half empty.

Liam let out a soft belch, tripped over Willow and lurched across the kitchen just as the back door opened. As he stumbled, his elbow caught the bowl of cake mix, and it slid across the counter. He dived for it, but it disappeared over the other side of the bench before he could save it. Grabbing the bench, he caught himself and stared at the visitor. Blue eyes full of amusement met his.

His groan echoed around the messy kitchen.

***

Angie had tried to call Liam on and off for the last few days. She had no news for him, but despite what she had told him about not calling unless she had anything to tell him, it was polite to let him know that she'd had no luck tracking down any local Boykin breeders. His phone had gone straight to an automatic voicemail service, and she was starting to think she may have taken the number down incorrectly. God knows, she'd been stressed enough when he'd given it to her at the Chinese restaurant, trying to find a way to tell him that Hugh was her friend's partner and not hers. Now that Liam was in town—or near town—it wouldn't hurt if he did think that. It would let her keep a bit of distance, and she hadn't lied. He'd come up with the idea when he'd talked to Hugh that night.

She'd been called out to the Ison farm to see to a horse with colic, and driving past Prickle Creek Farm on the way back, she'd decided, on the spur of the moment, to call in.

Willow was her patient, and that was the main reason she was visiting, she rationalised to herself, as the wheels clattered on the cattle grate at the edge of the Prickle Creek driveway.

Now she stood and surveyed Liam, the mess, and Willow, who was enthusiastically licking up whatever was smeared all over the floor.

Angie bent down and scooped up the little pup. 'Oh, no, you don't. You'll make yourself sick, little one.' She couldn't help the smile that tugged at her lips. Liam's white T-shirt was covered in blobs of what looked—and smelled like—chocolate cake mix. The same globs sat on the bench tops, the cupboard fronts and—she looked up in disbelief—the ceiling.

She tried to stifle the laugh that threatened, but it escaped her lips. 'Practising for Master Chef, are you?' Angie put one hand to her stomach as the laugh threatened to take over. 'What the heck are you doing?' She frowned and then sniffed as the smell of alcohol drifted across to her. Her gaze settled on the half-empty bottle of whisky on the kitchen sink and then moved back to Liam's face. There were more chocolate blobs in his hair, and a big one had dried on his cheek beneath his right eye.

'I'm making a chocolate cake for Lucy.' He straightened up, but the hiccup that came from his lips took away the gravity of his stance.

'That's very thoughtful of you. I heard she was coming home with the new bub today.'

'No. Not for Lucy. For Lucy.'

'How much of that bottle have you had to drink, Liam?'

'Not as much as it looks. Most of it is in here for the—*sshh*—secret ingredient.' He shrugged and held up a cup. 'What I mean is, it's not for Lucy, it's for the show. She couldn't make it for Gran, so I got volunteered.' A smile spread across his lips, and the glob of cake cracked and ran down his face. 'Can you cook cakes? I really could do with a hand here. I'm going to have to start again.'

Angie put the pup down on the floor and looked at Liam for a moment. 'I guess I can help out if you tell me what has to be done.'

She looked around the room with her hands on her hips. 'But first off, let's clean up this mess. Willow's going to be sick if she keeps licking the floor and how did you get cake mix on the ceiling?'

'Um. I sort of didn't put those beater things in the machine properly, and when they were at full speed, they came whirling out.' This time, his smile was cheeky. 'For a moment there, I thought I was going to lose my manhood. I had to jump out of the way of the whirling blades.'

'Too much information. Do you want me to help or not?'

'Yes, please.' A meek Liam was certainly not one Angie was used to.

##

Angie washed her hands and rolled up the sleeves of her shirt. Luckily, it seemed there was a spare cup of the 'secret ingredient' left for her to help Liam mix up another batch of chocolate cake. She couldn't help the grin as she looked at him. There was still a blob of chocolate mix on the tip of one ear, and his hair was standing in spikes on his head where he'd obviously rubbed his hand through it in frustration. She burst out laughing. 'Looks like you've invented a new hair product.'

'I'll give you some to take home if you want.' His grin was wide, and his eyes were dancing. Angie ignored the warm feeling in her chest and picked up the laminated recipe from the counter. She reached for a dishcloth and wiped the goo off the recipe.

'Okay, so if you're entering this in the show, you can mix it. I'll supervise.' She was looking forward to this. In London, Liam had been useless in the kitchen, and when it had been his turn to cook dinner, they'd always gone to the pub on the corner.

'Aw, come on, Angie, I've already made one. Can't you do it for me? Please? I can pass things to you.' The look on his face was just like the little pup at their feet.

This was a contrite Liam, very different from the one she had known. 'No.' She shook her head. 'I'll supervise. Now, is there an apron I can put on over my work clothes? They might look clean, but I've been out at the Isons' place with the horses.'

Angie was impressed when Liam opened a drawer and pulled one out. She shook her head. 'You really know your way around a kitchen these days.' Their eyes met and held as they both recalled his reluctance to cook in London.

'I've learned a lot of new skills in the last few months.'

She leaned forward as he slipped the apron over her head and stood still as Liam slipped his arms around her and tied the apron. Angie put her head down and absorbed his warmth as he stood close.

'And cake making is one of them?' The scepticism in her voice obviously had an effect.

Liam stepped back and nodded. 'Yes, it is. Anyone can follow a recipe. If I hadn't tripped over that damned dog—'

'If you hadn't been drinking the whisky, you might have been more stable on your feet.' Angie folded her arms. 'And I recall someone who couldn't even boil an egg. I guess living in the outback has improved your culinary skills.' Another giggle bubbled up from her chest, and he looked sheepish. 'And now here you are, cooking cakes for a competition. Come on, get out another bowl. The sooner you get this mixed, the sooner it will be in the oven.'

It was as though they'd never been away from each other. Angie perched on the stool as Liam weighed and measured and ensured that the beaters were firmly in the mixer before he turned it on. She grinned and shook her head when he tipped the cup of whisky into the mix, lifted one brow and held up the bottle.

'Can I interest you in a tipple, Ms Head Chef?'

'No, thank you. And you don't need any more either until that cake is baked. Not if you want to win.'

His brow creased in a frown. 'It has to win, Ange. I'm doing it for Gran.'

Angie slid off the stool and walked over to where he was peering into the bowl as though something was going to jump out and bite him. She peered into the bowl, put her hand on his shoulder and smiled. 'It looks perfect. You start clearing up and I'll put the mix in the cake tin and then in the oven for you.'

'You always were a good woman, Angie Edmonds.' A belch accompanied the words, and Angie rolled her eyes.

An hour later, the kitchen was spotless, Willow was asleep in her basket, and the tempting aroma of baking chocolate cake filled the house. Liam opened the fridge door and held up a bottle of wine, but Angie shook her head.

'A cup of tea,' she said firmly. 'I have to drive back to town.'

'You could always stay the night.' Liam looked at her sideways as he closed the fridge door.

She put the tea towel on the bench. 'Liam.' Her voice held a warning note.

'Come on, Ange. Where's your sense of fun gone?' Liam crossed to the sink and let the water out. 'I was teasing.'

She watched as the soapy water swirled down the sink. 'It wasn't funny.'

'Just a pleasant night chatting. The spare room is made up. I owe you for saving my neck. God forbid Gran's cake doesn't make the show,' he said.

'Don't count your chickens yet. The cake's not out of the oven. Things can still go wrong.' For a moment, she fought the urge to accept the offer of a drink and then shrugged. The thought of sitting, watching an outback sunset with Liam, sipping wine, was too tempting. 'All right, one glass and mix it with soda water. I won't stay for long, though; I'm going to call in at the Mackenzie farm on the way home. I have a little present for the baby, and I forgot to give it to Hugh.'

'Hugh? Who's Hugh?' Liam hiccupped again.

Heat ran up Angie's neck. 'I mean Garth.'

Liam looked at her curiously as he poured half a glass of wine. 'I'll come over to Lucy's place with you in your car if that's okay. Once the cake is out of the oven, that is.'

They sat out on the west-facing back verandah. Liam pushed the button to drop down the automated insect screens. The bugs were starting to come out as the warmer weather approached. Angie ignored the play of muscles beneath the clean T-shirt he had changed into while she'd cleaned up the mess in the kitchen. Liam had certainly built up in the months since she'd last seen him in London. She remembered how he had paid out on their friends who were gym junkies. Before she could stop herself, she asked, 'Do you keep in touch with Jimmy and Harriet?'

'What made you think of them?'

'Oh. Nothing.' She picked up her glass and took a sip. 'I just thought about them. I was remembering how they used to almost live at the gym.'

'No, I don't. They split up not long after you left. Harriet ran off with the guy who owned the gym.' The light was dim, and it was hard to see the expression on his face, but Liam's voice was soft. 'We had some fun times over there together, didn't we, Ange?'

'Yes, it was fun for a while.' This time, she held his stare and brought the subject back to the mundane. 'Although I don't miss the weather at all.'

'I missed you when you left, you know.'

Don't go there. Don't go there.

'I had to leave. My visa ran out. You didn't want to come. End of story.' Angie tipped the wine glass up and drained it in one long drink. 'Anyway, it's time for me to get going. If you want a lift over to Garth and Lucy's, I'm going now.'

Liam looked at her strangely. 'Don't you want to wait till the cake is done? It'll only be a few minutes now.'

In perfect synchronicity with his words, the oven timer bell rang. They both jumped up at the same time, and Liam grabbed for Angie as she tried to avoid touching him and overbalanced at the edge of the small table between their seats. Warm hands—newly callused hands—grabbed her bare arms, and she looked into the chest she had been admiring only moments ago. She fought the desire to rest her head on the clean, fresh-smelling T-shirt. She knew there was a perfect hollow at the base of his shoulder, where her head had rested many times. In happiness, in sadness, in frustration, and in friendship.

And in love.

God, she had loved this man. Had, that was the word she had to focus on. But he hadn't loved her. Or if he had, it hadn't been enough. Career one, love zero.

Wake up. You can't lose what you never had. Angie stood stiff and straight in his arms and didn't look up at Liam. Finally, he loosened his grip, and she slowly lifted her head.

No.

He was staring at her, and she knew that look in his eyes. She had seen it many times before, but in those days, she had been his partner, not someone he had let go because he hadn't loved her more than his career. Just like her dad hadn't loved Angie and her mum enough. He'd left and not missed them. Just like Liam had been unconcerned when she'd left. Now she was here and convenient for him, and it looked like he was going to take advantage of it.

Not on her life would she let him.

She widened her eyes, knowing she must look like a frightened rabbit caught in the headlights, but that didn't stop the slow and purposeful descent of his head. His lips stopped a whisker away from hers, and she held her breath. The soothing smell of whisky puffed from his mouth, warming her lips as he spoke.

'I don't suppose you'd let me kiss you. For old times' sake?'

She shoved her hands against his chest and forgot about the pleasure and the temptation of a whiskey-flavoured kiss. 'You suppose right, Liam Smythe. And I suggest, if you want the blue ribbon at the show, you get the cake out of the oven before it burns.'

'Burns! Would it really burn that quickly?'

'Yes, it would. And dry out, and crack.'

Angie followed his mad dash into the kitchen at a more sedate pace, taking advantage of the time to get her emotions back under control. She watched as he first picked up a tea towel and then a dishcloth before she took pity on him.

There was no need to be uncooperative just because he'd crossed a line.

'Get out of the way.' Angie nudged him aside with her hip, picked up the oven mitt, and carefully opened the oven. She couldn't help but smile. A perfect cake with a smooth oval top sat on the middle shelf. Not a crack to be seen. Liam hovered by her shoulder as she reached in and slid the oven mitt beneath it.

'Careful,' he said.

She nodded and carried it across to the sink and placed it on the stainless steel pad. 'Do you have a cake cooler?'

'A what?'

'Never mind. Where are the cake tins kept?'

'In the bottom of the pantry in the laundry.'

Angie started for the door but paused and turned around, lifting a finger at Liam. 'Don't touch it. Don't move, don't breathe near it, or it might sink in the middle. Or even worse, crack right across the top.'

In the pantry cupboard, beneath the cake tins, she found a stack of cake coolers, pulled one out and hurried back to the kitchen. He hadn't moved, but his expression was one of anxiety.

'God, this is worse than an editorial meeting at the paper. Much more stressful.'

She simply raised a brow, turning her attention to gently patting the cooling cake out onto the wire stand. It slipped out of the tin perfectly. Carefully, she pulled the circular ring of baking paper from the bottom of the cake. Not one crumb came away.

'You've done well,' she said.

'We've done well. Thank you. I couldn't have done it without you.'

Before Angie could move away, Liam leaned forward quickly and brushed his lips against hers. This time, she tasted the whisky on his breath.

Chapter Seven

Liam was more than pleased with the events of the day. The farm chores were caught up, Willow was almost recovered, the cake—the *perfect* cake—was cooling beneath a tea towel, and he was sitting beside Angie in her car heading over to the Mackenzie Farm.

'It's not too late to call in, I hope. I won't stay long. If Lucy's in bed, I'll just give the gift to Garth and head back to town.' Angie's voice was anxious, and Liam frowned. She'd never been a worrier before, and he hoped that he wasn't responsible for her jitteriness. She'd been so prickly since they'd met up in town. Even when they split up in London, she'd been sweet and gentle about it. Except for the night she'd left—she'd been quiet and had looked so lost when she'd got in that damn black cab.

And that had made him feel worse about the whole thing. She'd always been the peacemaker, and she had always been the one to draw him out of his bad moods. His frequent bad moods. Now that he was away from the newspaper world, he was beginning to realise how stressed he'd been and how hard it must have been for Angie to put up with him. Maybe that was why she hadn't pushed hard for him to come back home with her when her visa ran out.

His kiss today had only been a quick peck, a brief brush of her lips to say thank you. The problem was he'd wanted more, but he knew that wasn't fair. Angie was here, and he'd be heading back to the city soon. Wanting more and kissing her wasn't the right thing to do. And there was this new guy, Grant, to consider. He'd better treat her right, or he'd have Liam to answer to. As long as Angie was happy, that would have to be enough for him.

The dogs at the Mackenzie farm ran around the unfamiliar vehicle, barking and yapping. Angie climbed out and patted each of them in turn, and Liam watched, marvelling at her calm patience. They'd left Willow asleep in the basket in the laundry after Angie had taken a look at her. Willow was learning quickly that the laundry basket was her place. She would sit on her cute little butt and stare up at him with those huge brown eyes. When he nodded, she would follow him into the living room. It had to be a coincidence. A young pup surely couldn't learn so quickly. And Liam was surprised to discover that he actually enjoyed the pup's company. She took away that edge of loneliness since Gran and Pops had headed off on their travels, and Lucy had married Garth and moved to the Mackenzie farm.

'Liam. Angie. Come on in. We've just made a cuppa.' Garth opened the screen door with a wide smile as they stepped onto the wide back veranda.

'No, I won't come in. I don't want to intrude. I just wanted to give you this.' Angie pressed a small parcel wrapped in white tissue paper into Garth's hand. She shot a look at Liam. 'I have to get back to town.'

'No, don't be silly. Come inside, both of you. At least meet Lucy before you go. You haven't met her, have you, Angie? She's holding court in the living room with Mum and Dad hanging off her every word. She's taken to being a mum like a champion.' Garth's chest puffed out, and Liam smiled. Fatherhood suited Garth.

Angie and Liam followed Garth through the house. He quickly introduced Angie to his parents before he led her over to Lucy and James.

A strange lump settled in Liam's throat as he watched Angie smile at Lucy and the baby.

'Our new vet, Luce. Angie Edmonds.' Garth nodded at Angie

as he introduced her.

Lucy's eyes widened and shifted across to meet Liam's briefly before she smiled and turned back to Angie. 'Hi, Angie. Pleased to meet you.'

Oh no! She'd remembered Angie's name. Liam shook his head at Lucy behind Angie's back. He'd spilled his guts to Lucy a few months ago when she had been despairing over Garth, and kidding herself she could go back to the city. Liam had told her about Angie and how much he regretted letting her go.

He couldn't believe he'd told Lucy, but he'd never even told Angie.

Lucy opened her mouth, but Liam caught her eye and shook his head again. She understood and cleared her throat. 'How thoughtful of you to bring a gift. How do you like Prickle Creek, Angie?'

'It's great,' Angie said. 'I'm a country girl. I grew up in rural Victoria, so I feel right at home.' She raised her hands, palms up. 'But the practice has been really busy; I've barely been able to get to know anyone in town yet.'

'Well, we'll have to do something about that, won't we?' Lucy smiled widely. 'I can think of a couple of things. The agricultural show is coming up, and we'll start having a few weekend dos out here now that summer is coming. I'll introduce you to all the locals.'

Liam almost rolled his eyes; Lucy was up to something. He could see it in her expression as she shifted her glance from him and then back to Angie. 'I thought you'd be too busy at home with young James to get involved in anything yet,' Liam said.

'No. I'm not going to be one of those stay-at-home mums. Plus, I've picked up some more freelance work from my boss in Sydney, too.'

'You are going to be busy.' Her mother-in-law's voice held a tinge of disapproval.

'I sure am. Now, Angie, would you be interested in helping me on some of my committees in town?'

'I'd love to help out. But let's talk about it another time. You've got visitors, and I really have to go now.' Angie turned to Liam. 'Do you want a lift home, or are you going to stay here?'

'Liam, you can stay for dinner.' Lucy's voice interrupted them. 'Garth can run you over to Prickle Creek Farm later.'

'Thanks for organising me, Lucy, but I'm quite capable of making my own decisions.' Liam burred up, but Lucy waved his protests away. 'No, I need to talk to you about the cake.'

'Ah, the cake.' A smile accompanied Angie's words, and the sweetness of that smile hit Liam right in the solar plexus. 'Liam's cake turned out beautifully. I'm looking forward to seeing how well he ices it,' she said.

Lucy looked from one to the other again. 'So you've been over at Gran and Pop's farm, Angie?

Angie's response sent any sweetness flying out the window. 'Only to see to Liam's new pup.'

So he didn't count in the scheme of things. Liam knew where he stood. Angie had a new partner—the wonderful Grant. And the only reason she'd called into the farm was in a professional capacity. He lifted his chin and he knew his expression was sour. 'Dinner sounds great, thanks Luce.'

Good manners dictated he should see Angie out, so he waited until she and Lucy had exchanged mobile numbers. 'You don't want to be too late driving back into town, Angie. The roos will be out and about,' he said.

'Yes, I know. I grew up in the country, remember?'

Does she ever lose that sweet, calm expression?

'I'm going now. Lovely to meet you, Lucy. I'll look forward to a coffee next time you're in town.' Angie took her car keys from her pocket, and Liam's head started to pound as he walked her to the back door.

The whiskey? Or the fact that he knew he had made a huge mistake letting her go?

Liam watched the tail lights of Angie's four-wheel-drive truck until they disappeared over the slight incline at the front gate of the Mackenzie farm. Angie had been polite but distant as he'd seen her to the vehicle. She was friendly with everyone else, but when she talked to him, it was as though she was putting a wall up between them. When she'd been in the kitchen helping with the cake, it had been like two friends spending time together. But she'd still held that air of fragility that had brought out his protective instinct when he'd first met her. She was putting on a tough act, and he wanted to know why. Liam was thoughtful as he turned to go back inside, but before he reached the house, the screen door creaked open, and Lucy came out onto the veranda.

'Lucy. What are you doing out here? Shouldn't you be sitting down?' Liam hurried across to her and took her arm.

'Gosh, Liam. I'm not sick. I gave birth. A week ago.'

'Okay, if you're sure.'

'Don't be silly. Men! I wanted to talk to you in private.' Lucy let Liam take her arm, and he led her over to the double bench at the end of the veranda overlooking the house paddock. He sat beside her and made sure she was comfortable on the soft cushions.

'Are you comfortable?'

'I'm fine! I wanted to ask you about—'

'The cake? It's fine. But I might need you to help me with the icing. Maybe I could bring it over here?'

'No, not the cake. Angie. I'm not mistaken, am I? Angie is your Angie from England?'

Liam dropped his hands between his knees and leaned

forward, staring at the wooden floorboards.

My Angie. She had been that for almost two years. His Angie and he'd blown it.

'No, not my Angie. But yes. Angie from England.'

Lucy made a rude sound. 'If I remember correctly, when you were giving me the wake-up call about being in love with Garth, you told me you were in love with her, and she came home.'

'Maybe.'

'There was no maybe about it. So now I'm giving you the talk. She seems lovely, and she's back here, so what are you going to do about it?'

'Nothing. One, she has a new guy in her life. And two, I'm only here till Sebastian and Jemima come and take over. Then I'm off to Sydney after Christmas. ABC, here I come.'

'Oh, Liam.' Lucy shook her head and put her hand on his arm, sympathy clouding her eyes. 'Are you really sure that's what you want? To go back to the city? You seem so happy and settled out here. Farm life suits you.'

'I am loving it, Luce. Because it's a working holiday. I need to get back to the real world.' Liam lifted his head and stared over the paddocks. 'My need to go to the city is different to what yours was. I'm not making a difference out here. Sure, I love the work and the lifestyle, and I love being on the farm—I can't think of a place I would rather live. But I need to be doing something worthwhile. Go back to investigating and reporting social issues. I've got my hopes pinned on the Sydney job, but I've also made enquiries in Brisbane and Melbourne. It's surprising how much work is around at the moment.'

'You have to go to the city to do something worthwhile? And there are no social issues out here in the outback? Do you think we live in fairyland? You disappoint me, Liam. You woke me up to myself; now I'm going to do the same for you. I heard the way you talked about Angie.' Lucy's grip on his arm tightened. 'I see the way you look at her. I can hear it in your voice now.'

'It's too late. She has a new partner.' His voice was flat. 'And a practice here, too.'

'Stay here. Fight for her.'

'What? So we get back together for a while, and then when I go back to work, we go our separate ways again.' Liam shook his head.

'Bloody hell, you were never a quitter.' Lucy stood up, and her ponytail swished from side to side as she turned to him. 'Promise me you'll think about it. Or I might have to throw in a helping hand.'

'Lucy,' Liam warned her. 'Don't interfere. Okay?'

'I'll see. Now tell me all about this cake.' She slipped her arm through his as they walked back inside.

Chapter Eight

Nothing had gone right today for Angie. The steriliser in the surgery had given up the ghost, and they were waiting on a rush order from Sydney, but the supplier had said it would be at least three days before they could send a replacement. So, all surgery had to be put on hold until it arrived. She would have to send any urgent cases to Coonamble or Narrabri. There had been a spate of sick dogs over the past couple of days, and she suspected they had been poisoned. The strange thing was, it was domestic pets from town, as well as a couple of kelpies from farms that were a long way out. Maybe it was a virus.

Cissy had taken ill after lunch, the casual vet nurse had been unavailable, and Angie had worked alone in the surgery and run off her feet. The last patient left, and she was about to pull the blind down and turn the closed sign around when a ute turned into the car park.

Oh, just fine and dandy. What did he want? Being so busy, she'd managed to put Liam out of her mind all day. Spending time with him yesterday—and helping him cook that damned cake— had led to a sleepless night. And seeing him with his family had made her feel extra lonely. She had vowed to herself to stay away from him, and then she would be able to survive until he left town to go back to his career.

She ignored the little shaft of pleasure that lodged in her chest when he got out of his ute. Obviously freshly showered and wearing clean jeans and a white T-shirt, he oozed manliness. *Damn him.*

She quickly turned the closed sign around and went to move back behind the counter; maybe he'd think she'd gone home already.

Coward.

All thoughts of not answering the door disappeared when Liam called out, and she peered through the gap in the sign. He cradled a limp little brown pup in his arms.

'Ange, are you in there?'

She flipped the lock over.

'Liam, come in. You just caught me. Oh no, don't tell me Willow is sick, too?'

He nodded, and his face was strained. 'Yes, when I came in from the paddock for smoko, she was quiet, and she's gone downhill quickly. I tried to ring, but the phone didn't pick up.'

'Sorry. I've been run off my feet. Cissy's sick'—she lifted her gaze to meet his—'and I've had a spate of sick dogs coming in all day.'

She gently took Willow from his arms and proceeded into the examination room, with Liam following closely behind. On the way, Angie grabbed a thermometer.

'Her temp is up, and she's beginning to show signs of dehydration.' Angie held up the thermometer and frowned. She checked the puppy's heart and respiration, looked in Willow's mouth, palpated the abdomen, checked for dehydration, and performed a rectal exam.

Liam stood beside her silently, clenching his baseball cap in his hands.

'I'll get her on a drip, and I'll take some bloods. I don't think it's parvovirus, but given that we don't know her history or if she's already had her vaccinations, we have to consider it.'

'That's bad, isn't it? For a little puppy like Willow?' Liam's voice was low as if the pup could understand what he was saying.

'It is, but I don't think it is parvo. The outbreak in all the dogs today makes me think it's another virus they've all picked up. Or they've been poisoned. The others have all been vaccinated against parvo, and they're all displaying the same symptoms as Willow. Has she been outside at all where she could have taken a bait?'

Liam shook his head. 'No, not at all. So probably not parvo?'

'Probably not, but she's still a very sick little girl.' Angie sighed. She was reluctant to put Willow out back with the other sick dogs in case she caught the virus from them. And besides, the cages were all taken. 'I'll take her home with me and put her on a drip at my place.' She handed Willow back to Liam and quickly cleaned down the examination table. 'Come on, it's only a short walk. I live two houses away.'

***

Angie held the door open for Liam as he stepped through with Willow, and he followed her as she headed down the footpath to the last house in the street. Willow was limp and panting in his arms. Angie smoothed her hand over the pup's head as they walked quickly to her house.

So much for my plan of staying away from her; it looked like Willow had other plans for him. He wondered how long it would have been before he had known that Angie was in town if Willow hadn't appeared at his front gate. Maybe he wouldn't have seen her again before he went back to Sydney. Maybe that would have been best. Certainly best for his peace of mind and certainly for his ability to sleep at night.

Half an hour later, Willow was asleep in a dog enclosure and being rehydrated.

'Thanks, Angie.' He couldn't help himself; he reached out and tucked a loose strand of hair behind her ear. It was just like old habits coming back. 'You look exhausted.'

'I am. It's been a big day. I'll have to call in one of the nurses from Coonamble if Cissy is still sick tomorrow.'

'Why don't you go take a shower, and I'll sit with Willow. And I'll order in some Chinese for us.'

'Chinese again?' Angie smiled, and her whole face glowed with life. Liam clenched his hands by his side as his heart warmed. All he wanted to do was take her in his arms and hold her close, but that right wasn't his anymore. She belonged to someone else now.

'Or does a hamburger hold more appeal?' He looked at his watch. 'The milk bar will still be taking orders, but we'll have to be quick.'

'Liam. You don't have to feed me.'

'Yes, I do.' He folded his arms. 'You have to eat. I have to eat. Someone has to watch Willow for a while.'

'All right,' she said slowly, but Liam sensed her hesitation. 'A hamburger would be good. Thank you.'

He reached out and gently held the top of her arms, then looked at his hands on her bare skin and quickly dropped them. He turned around and ran his hand through his hair in frustration. 'I'm sorry. That just came naturally.'

'It's okay.' Angie lifted her head and held his gaze, her pale blue eyes holding his. 'It's an awkward situation. We seem to be thrown together a lot recently. But it's okay. We can be friends.'

That's not what he wanted, but the offer of friendship would do for a start. Maybe as friends, he would have the right to probe a bit more about this new man of hers. See how serious it was. See if he had a chance.

Damn fool. Even if he did have a chance, there was no point. He was leaving soon. Her life was here. His was away.

'Ironic, isn't it?' The words were out before he could think. 'Last time you had to leave. This time, it's me.'

'Yes, it is.' Angie's voice was hard to read as she turned away and checked on Willow. 'You go and get some dinner.

Willow will be fine while I take a shower. Then I'll have to go back to the surgery and check on my other patients.'

'Would it help if I came, too?'

'It would, but I wouldn't ask you to. It means cleaning out some nasty messes in the cages.'

Liam laughed. 'You might get a surprise, Ange. Farmer Liam is a bit different to the bloke I was in London.'

This time, it was Angie who put a hand on his arm. He resisted the temptation to put his hand over hers.

'I like both Liam's,' she said. 'But if Farmer Liam'—her eyes crinkled in a smile—'is willing to hose out some smelly cages, I would be most grateful.'

'One condition.' He matched her smile. 'We eat first because I don't think I'll keep my appetite after doing that!'

##

A couple of hours later, as Angie locked the door of the surgery behind them, Liam wondered if he would be able to keep his hamburger and chips down. He'd had no idea what Angie's job entailed. When they'd lived together in London, he'd been selfish. All the times that she'd asked him to come along and see where she worked, he'd always had an excuse at the ready. He guessed he'd thought that her work was like a doctor's, and someone else did the messy stuff. He'd been too full of his career and his own self-importance to take the time to see what she did. No wonder she'd taken off when she had the chance.

The mess they had cleaned up tonight had made him gag a few times, but Angie had been patient and had spoken lovingly to each of the dogs after the cages were cleaned.

'I really do appreciate the hand you gave me tonight,' she said.

'I guess we're even now. You helped me with the cake, and I returned the favour.'

'Yep, we're square, and I think the dogs are all improving.' Angie shivered and rubbed her arms as they walked along the road to her house. 'Still a touch of the west in that spring wind.'

The night had come in quickly, and a cool breeze was blowing from the north. Above them, the stars shone like diamonds, peppering the night sky with shards of brilliant light. Liam still couldn't get over the difference in the night sky out here from the city.

'It's fresh tonight. I hope Willow has improved, too.'

Angie pushed open her front door. 'Me, too.'

'Don't you lock your door?' Liam frowned.

'No need to out here.'

'I beg to disagree. Just because you're in the bush doesn't mean it's suddenly safe.'

'Don't start telling me what to do, Liam.' Her voice held a warning tone.

'Just looking out for you.'

'I'm quite capable of doing that myself. I've gotten used to being alone.' She stumbled over her words.

Liam pulled back before she lost her cool. 'Whatever. I'll just take a look at Willow before I go home.'

The atmosphere was tense as they walked into the small enclosed veranda at the back of Angie's house. The easy camaraderie that had been there as they'd eaten hamburgers and then worked together at the surgery had disappeared.

Willow was sitting up, looking out through the cage. When she saw them, her little tail thumped, and she tried to stand up.

'Well, that's a lovely sight,' Liam said. He reached in through the cage, and Willow licked his hand. He felt her nose; it was cold and wet again.

'Definitely not parvovirus.' Angie's voice was brisk and professional. 'She would have gone downhill without medication.

Looks like she's got what the others have. Whatever it is.' She turned to Liam and folded her arms. 'I'll keep her here overnight, and if she's still good in the morning, you can take her back home. I meant to tell you, too, I've had no luck finding anyone who lost a pup. She must have been dumped.'

'It's hard to understand how anyone would do that, isn't it?' Liam felt as though he'd been dismissed, so he quickly said, 'Thanks. You're a great vet.'

'Thank you.' It was hard to read her tone.

'I mean it, I'm sorry I didn't appreciate what you did when we were in London.' He gave Willow one last tickle beneath her chin. 'I'll come in about lunchtime tomorrow if that's okay. I've got a cattle truck coming, and I have to load a couple of dozen heifers.

'I really can't get used to this new you.' This time, Angie smiled. 'Whenever you can make it in is fine. If there's any change in her condition, I'll give you a call. Give me your number again. I think I got it wrong last time.' She shook her head as she pulled out her phone and updated Liam's contact as he gave her the number again. Angie walked to the door with him.

'Bye, then.' A moment of awkwardness hovered as Liam shoved his hands in his pocket. He fought the automatic reflex to kiss her goodbye. You couldn't live with someone for two years, and not have little habits or rituals that came naturally.

'Goodbye,' she said. Before he could say anything more, the front door closed gently.

Liam walked back to the car park of the surgery to collect his car.

Chapter Nine

Angie's buzzing phone woke her just after seven the next morning, and she groaned.

Please don't be Cissy calling in sick again.

She'd have to get her skates on to get to the surgery in time. Picking up the phone, she yawned and opened her messages as she swung her legs over the side of the bed. There were two messages; she must have been so deeply asleep that she'd only heard the last one beep in.

The first one was from Cissy, saying she'd be in for work today. *Thank goodness.*

The second one was from Lucy asking if it was okay to add Angie's name to the helper's roster for the Prickle Creek Agricultural Show next weekend.

She quickly responded to Lucy's text.

Sure, prefer afternoon Saturday or anytime Sunday.

Angie checked on Willow, who was now standing on her back legs, front paws resting on the middle of the cage. 'Well, look who's all better.' Before she headed for the shower, she served out a very small portion of boiled rice and chicken protein mix to see how Willow fared with that. The small pup wolfed it down and then curled up for a sleep. Angie picked up her phone and hesitated as she clicked on, *compose new message.*

Go on, she thought. Liam will be worried.

Willow much better, she typed. Her finger hovered over the keys. In the old days, they had always sent long and funny texts to each other. She took a deep breath and pressed send. Those days were gone.

When she was in the shower, Angie tipped her head back

and let the warm water soothe her. Her sleep had been fitful, and when she had finally dozed off, Liam had filled her dreams for the fifth night in a row. Last night, they'd been back in London, walking around the streets holding hands. Then he'd disappeared, and she'd run around trying to find him. She'd been annoyed that her cheeks had been damp with tears when she'd woken up in the middle of the night. It had taken ages to get back to sleep.

As soon as Liam collected Willow, she was going to do everything she could to avoid him. Her feelings for him were rushing back like a freight train. Eating hamburgers with him last night and working side-by-side in the surgery had been satisfying—you couldn't call it fun—not with some of those messes he'd helped hose out. But it had been too chummy, and old habits had kicked in. She'd gotten the salt shaker out of the cupboard and was salting his chips before she even realised what she was doing. Her hamburger had been perfect—no onion and double cheese with chilli sauce. Just like Liam knew she liked it.

They couldn't go on this way. Angie wasn't strong enough to be left behind when he hightailed it to Sydney.

Even though, through dinner and the cage scrubbing, he'd been kind and interested in her well-being. That apology for not appreciating her in London had filled her with warmth. It had come from his heart. If he'd been like that in London, she would have begged him to come home with her—but she was getting ahead of herself. Just because he now appreciated what she did—and did well—didn't mean that they were going to get back together.

As far as Liam knew, she had Gary, Greg, or Grant—or whatever her fictional fiancé's name was. And Liam would be leaving at Christmas. Only a few weeks away.

It would be better all round if they only saw each other when it was absolutely necessary. When he came to pick Willow up, she'd make sure Cissy took him over to the house. Vet and client relationship—that's all they had. And that's all they *would* have from now on.

As she rinsed the shampoo from her hair, Angie blocked the image of Liam cooking his chocolate cake. It made her feel altogether too warm and fuzzy. She needed to be strong. Last night, he'd been thinking of kissing her goodbye. She knew him well enough to see the intent in his eyes.

She loved him enough to let him do it. As the water ran down her face, she knew some of it was from the tears spilling from her eyes. After the show next weekend, she'd get a locum in and go and pretend to visit Grant for a while. She hadn't caught up with Jenny for ages.

***

On the way to town, after the heifers had been rounded up and loaded onto the truck, Liam swung by the Mackenzie farm. He'd gotten into that habit since Lucy had moved over there. Invariably, she needed something from town, and he'd enjoyed sitting on the veranda with her as her pregnancy progressed. He slammed the door of the ute, climbed up the steps, and stood at the back door.

'Luce? You home?'

'Come through, Liam. I'm on the front veranda.'

'Do you want me to make a cuppa on the way through?'

'Yes, please.'

Five minutes later, he juggled two cups of tea and a plate of homemade bickies as he walked down the timber floor of the hall. He looked around with admiration. Garth had designed and built this house before Lucy had come back to Prickle Farm last year, and he'd done a superb job. It was almost a Japanese minimalist style—the last thing you'd expect to see in a farmhouse. Liam looked around enviously. It would be good to create something like this and have a place you could call your own.

Out here on the farm. He'd build it overlooking the back bore. There was a good view of the mountains in the distance from there.

He shook his head, and the tea slopped over his hand. *God, what's getting into me? I'm not staying here, so why on earth would I think about building a house here?*

'What are you looking so worried about?' Lucy was sitting in an old rocking chair, and James was asleep in the pram beside her.

'Nothing.' Telling Lucy what he was thinking would be tantamount to telling her she knew what was best for him. He passed her a cup of tea and took two biscuits from the plate before he put it on the small table between the chairs. 'Need anything in town?'

'No, thanks. Garth took a list to Narrabri with him. He's taken his parents back to the airport.'

'That was a quick visit.'

'They're good in-laws. Susan said they didn't want to overstay their welcome, though I have to learn to be more patient with her when she tries to tell me what to do.'

'A bit of your own medicine.' Liam couldn't help adding. Lucy smiled.

The silence was companionable as they looked out over the paddocks.

'What do you have to go to town for?' Lucy reached over and patted the baby's back as he began to stir.

'Have to go to the vet's. Willow got sick last night.'

'Oh, that's nice.' Lucy smiled like a cat that got the cream.

'No, it's not. Poor Willow was really crook. She could have died.'

She waved a hand. 'I didn't mean that. I meant it was nice that you were seeing Angie again.'

'Lucy.'

'I like her. And I can see why you loved—love—her.'

'Lucy, drop it.' Liam held his temper, keeping his voice low so he didn't wake the baby. 'It's over, okay? Angie has moved on, and I'm moving away. And since you are so concerned about my dog, yes, Willow is fine. Angie sent a text.'

'Okay.'

He looked at her suspiciously as she acquiesced.

'So how did the icing go? You didn't ring me.'

Liam felt his mouth drop open. 'Oh, shit. I forgot all about icing the cake.'

'The damn cake.' Lucy smiled, and he forgave her for being persistent about Angie. 'Bring it over here, and we can do it together later. It has to be in town by tomorrow for the judging. And that's what else I wanted to ask you. Can I put you on the roster to help out at the show next weekend?'

'I don't know if I'll have time. Especially with another trip into town tomorrow.'

'Come on, where's your community spirit?' Lucy's smile was innocent.

'In the cattle crush, in the irrigation pipes, and all the other places where I have chores banked up.'

'I told you, Garth can come over and help you out.'

'All right. Add me to the roster, you witch. You always get what you want, anyway.' He nudged her with his elbow. 'Always did, ever since you were a little girl. You really are a chip off Gran's old block.'

'I hope so.' Again, the innocent smile. 'She's a good person.'

Liam stood and gathered the cups. 'I'll come back over at teatime, and we'll ice that damn cake together.'

Lucy's laughter pealed out.

'What's so funny?'

'Did you read the end of the recipe?'

'No,' he said. 'Why?'

'You'll see.'

'If anyone had ever told me coming home to Prickle Creek Farm would see me cooking and icing cakes, there is no way I would have ever left England.'

Lucy stood and hugged him. 'But you did, and you're doing very well. And you know what? To be honest, I really think you should consider staying here. Gran and Pop reckon you are. I know you just said that so they'd enjoy their trip, but Liam, do something for me?'

'What's that?'

'Give it some thought.'

'Maybe.'

Not in a million years.

An hour later, Liam was on his way back to the farm with Willow curled up in a box on the seat beside him. To his disappointment, there'd been no sign of Angie, and Cissy had taken him to the house and bailed Willow out of the cage. The little spaniel had almost wagged her tail off when she'd spotted him, and Liam hadn't been able to help the smile that came to his lips.

'So, how was Angie this morning, Willow?' Liam shook his head and turned the radio to the country and western station. Not only did he have a pretty pup, a non-working dog, now he was talking to the damn thing. He turned the volume up, and the next time he looked across at Willow, she was curled up asleep in the box.

Yep, Smythe. You are getting soft. It was past time to start looking for a job back in the city.

Chapter Ten

Liam smiled when he read Gran's icing recipe in Lucy's kitchen that evening. *Ice the Damn Cake* was at the top of the instructions. James cooperated by staying asleep, and he watched as Lucy twirled the finishing touch on the icing with a flat knife.

'There's no way I could have done that,' he said.

'Really?' Lucy licked the last of the icing off the spatula. 'I heard you say that about the cattle work when we first came home. Amazing the new skills you've picked up this year.'

'Look who's talking,' Liam teased back. 'Whoever would have thought you'd pick up all these new skills when we came back?'

Lucy held up the spatula, and her nose wrinkled in a frown. 'What, making cakes?'

'No, silly. Being a wife and mother.'

'Never in a million years did I think I wanted that. Amazing what true love does, isn't it?' Her grin was fast and cheeky. 'There's hope for you yet. We'll have to look for a wife for you. To get you to stay here. I'd miss you if you went, and so would Garth.' Her grin widened. 'And so would Ang—'

'I'm going to see Garth about the cattle work next week.' Liam cut her short and turned on his heel. He headed for the side door where Garth was sitting on the veranda having a beer. He glanced back before he went outside and saw the look on Lucy's face. She was up to something.

'Don't you even think about matchmaking, Lucy, or I'll go back to Sydney sooner than you can say snap. You can look after Gran and Pop's farm until Sebastian and Jemima arrive.' He wasn't fast enough to look back at her, but he'd swear that he caught a glimpse of Lucy poking her tongue out at him.

'Don't forget you have a child to set an example to now, smart arse,' he shot back.

'Come on, you pair, stop fighting. You're worse than a brother and sister.' Garth reached down into the cooler beside his chair and passed Liam a beer. 'Pull up a pew, mate. You look like you could do with a drink.'

'Thanks.' Liam reached for the beer and sat in the chair opposite Garth. 'Lucy said you might be able to spare me some time over the weekend.'

'For sure.' Garth nodded. 'Where do you need help?'

'You name it, I'm behind in everything, but if you could help me drench the cattle from the front paddock, that would be great.'

'Sunday morning suit?'

'Perfect. Appreciate it.' Liam tipped his beer up and let the cool liquid run down his throat; it barely touched the sides. Summer was approaching fast, and when the cool westerly eased off, the temperature got hotter each day.

'I was in town this afternoon and ran into Jim Ison. He said you were going to help with the alliance.' Garth put his empty beer bottle on the floor. 'I've signed up, too. He asked me to tell you there's a community meeting on Monday. Having you on board will be awesome.'

'You really think I can help much? I don't know a lot about the water table out here. Just what we learned at school.'

'You don't need to, mate. There are enough of us out here who can talk about the dangers to the water supply if this coal seam gas mining goes ahead. With your newspaper connections, Jim reckons we'll be able to get some inside info on the company that's behind it. That will get us on the front foot.'

'I'll give Jim a call tonight when I get home. It would

probably help if I had some data to bring along to the meeting.' Liam's journalistic nose began to itch. It would be great to get his head around something apart from cattle weights, drenches, and puppies.

And Angie. He pushed that thought away.

'Busy few weeks coming up. The alliance campaign, the show, and the christening in the New Year. And Lucy's organising a huge Christmas do because everyone will be home.' Garth leaned forward. 'Got a big favour to ask you, mate.'

'What's that?'

'How would you feel about being James's godfather?'

'Wow, Garth, for real? I'd be stoked.'

'I don't have any brothers, and you're as close to Lucy as a brother. The way you two blue with each other, you might as well be.' Garth held out his hand, and as Liam shook it, he called out to Lucy. 'We have a godfather, sweetheart.'

Liam stood and picked up the two empty beer bottles as Lucy stepped onto the veranda.

'That's great news. Jemmy already said yes to being James's godmother.' She stood on her toes and kissed Liam's cheek. 'Thank you.'

'What about Seb?' Liam asked.

'He's lined up for the next one, he promised.' Lucy sat in the chair that Liam had vacated.

'So, is this cake ready to go?' he asked. 'Where do I have to take it to?'

'I rang Sally Ison. She and the rest of the committee are meeting at the showground tomorrow to start the judging, so she said if you get into town after ten, you can take it straight to the pavilion where the baked goods will be on display.'

'And that's the last time I'm going to town for a week.'

Garth grinned at him. 'No, it's not. You've got the alliance meeting on Monday.'

'Jeez, I am getting to know that road very well.' Liam groaned and headed for the kitchen. 'I hope you've packed this cake securely.'

'It's in Gran's Tupperware cake holder, and it won't slide. But still, drive carefully. You take care of it and make sure you get it in tomorrow afternoon. Gran's record is depending on you.'

He saluted her, and she shook her head as he walked to the gate carrying the cake container.

'And don't forget about it and leave it in the car,' Lucy called after him.

'Yes, ma'am.'

Liam drove home through the back gate very sedately, the iced chocolate cake perched in pride of place in the middle of the back seat.

***

Angie's week improved after the weekend. Cissy was back on deck, all of the sick dogs had recovered and gone back to their owners, and with the preparation for the Prickle Creek Agricultural Show well underway, business was quiet. They got all of the new signs up, and as she stood back and looked at the sign that displayed Dr. Angie Edmonds, Veterinary Surgeon, in large black letters, a surge of pride flooded through her. Mum would have been so proud. She had sacrificed so much so that Angie could go to university in Melbourne, but she had died the year before Angie had graduated. That was one of the reasons she had gone to England on the veterinary exchange. Mum's death had left such a hole in her life she'd thought a change of scene would help her get over the grief.

It had helped a little bit, and then she'd met Liam not long after she had arrived. It hadn't taken long for them to discover they had the loss of their mothers in common. He'd asked her out for dinner the next night, and they'd been a couple almost from then on.

When she'd come back to Australia, Angie had carried a different sort of loss. Sadness for a lost relationship and knowing that Liam had cared more about his job than whatever it was they'd had together. It had sucked, but that's the way it was. The only thing she was thankful for was that she had never said those three little words to him. Although God knows, many times she'd been so close to saying 'I love you.' The weekend he had taken her to Paris, the Sunday he had come off the cricket field after hitting the winning run, and that night they'd had a candlelit dinner by the Thames. Each time, her heart had been filled with love for him, and she'd almost said it. They'd had such wonderful times together. She closed her eyes and was transported back to Paris. Liam had stood behind her on the riverboat as they'd taken a trip down the Seine. She could still feel his arms around her waist as she leaned back against his firm chest and the whisper of his breath as he murmured sweet nothings into her ear. He had been so romantic. When had it all stopped?

Had he lost interest in her as time had passed? Had it happened before she'd come home to their flat that night and announced she had to go home before the winter came? She'd given it no thought; she'd been so sure that he would come go home with her.

The wind was icy as she made her way up the street, the first night when one knew the northern hemisphere winter was on the way. The sky was heavy, the wind gusting, as she picked up dinner at the local curry house around the corner from their third-floor flat.

'I'm home,' she called as she pushed the door open, balancing the curry in one hand and her keys in the other.

'I'm in the study,' he called out. Angie remembered

smiling. What Liam called his study was a small space at the end of their wardrobe before you climbed up the one step to the postage stamp-sized bathroom.

'You're late,' he said as she dropped a kiss on his cheek and then pulled her boots off.

'The first train was full. I had to wait for the late one.' Angie yawned. 'God, I had such a busy day.'

'Mm.' Liam's attention was on the computer screen in front of him. 'Dinner smells good.'

'Come and wash up. I need to talk to you. I got a letter today.'

Ten minutes later, they sat side-by-side at the small table squeezed into the kitchen.

'What letter?' he asked as he scraped his plate clean.

Angie picked at her dinner, her appetite gone. As Liam ate, she began to worry. What if he decided to stay when she left? Her work visa was about to expire. He had managed to renew his, but she was on a work exchange program with no option to renew. She'd tried her best for an extension, but today's letter had advised that her visa was definitely not eligible for renewal.

'I have to go home before the end of May. There's no way out.'

As soon as she saw his expression close, Angie knew. He was going to stay. She wasn't important enough in his life for him to come back to Australia with her.

She would be going home alone. Their romantic interlude— the situation she had foolishly kidded herself would turn into something permanent—was over.

##

As she scrubbed out the sinks in the surgery, Liam and those romantic days wouldn't stay out of her mind. There was one thing she had to keep in the forefront of her mind. She was kidding herself if she thought there was any future in the attention he was paying her now. It was just because she was here… and convenient. He hadn't searched her out when he'd come back. He had her email address. Although, to be fair to him—if she had to be—Liam was keeping his distance now—most of the time—because he thought she had a new man in her life. She really needed to sort that out, but there never seemed to be a good time, and the longer she left it, the more it looked like she'd set up a deliberate lie. It had started as a simple misunderstanding that had gotten out of hand. And if she told him now, he'd think that maybe she was hoping they could take up where they'd left off in London. And that wasn't going to happen.

I'm not going to have my heart broken a second time.

She'd loved Liam. Maybe he had cared about her in his own way, but he'd loved his job more. The good times they'd had together in London had been fun, but in the end, he'd made his choice. And she'd come back home and got on with her life.

It was nothing like when her dad had left her and Mum. Tears pricked at Angie's eyes as she remembered how devastated Mum had been the night he'd walked out. Mum had never shared with her why he did it or what the problem was, so of course, Angie blamed herself. Even though she had been a young child, she'd been old enough to understand the emotion that had died in their family. Dad had stopped teasing her and taking her to Saturday softball. She'd heard the arguments, and she'd blamed herself.

Her resolve hardened as she scrubbed the sink so vigorously that the stainless steel pad went flying across the tiles.

'No more,' she muttered as she picked up the pad and resumed scrubbing. No matter how much Liam tried to sweet-talk her, she would stay heart whole this time.

Dr Angie Edmonds was an independent and confident

woman. That would be her new mantra. She'd do a poster, put the affirmation on her fridge, and recite it every morning. She wasn't going to be available for Liam to fill his time with until he went off to the city to take up his career again.

No way.

Scrub, scrub, scrub.

At this rate, her fingertips would be scoured away even with rubber gloves on. The pad went flying again as Cissy walked in, her arms laden with a delivery that had just arrived. 'Wow, I've never seen those sinks so shiny,' she exclaimed. 'They look brand new.'

Angie smiled. 'They do, don't they?'

'While I think of it, Sally Ison rang before. She asked if you could call her back.'

'No appointments called in?' Angie pulled off the rubber gloves.

'No, we have a clear afternoon.'

'Great. I'll call Sally now.' She walked back into the reception area as a white Nissan ute cruised slowly down the road. Her heart notched up a few beats, and she strolled casually over to the window next to the pet food shelf. She bent down and peered through it.

It wasn't Liam's ute. Feeling cross with herself, she went back to the counter and picked up the phone. The sooner she got that affirmation up on her fridge, the better.

'Independence and confidence,' she muttered under her breath as she dialled the phone.

'Hi Sally, it's Angie Edmonds here. You wanted to talk to me?'

Five minutes later, not only was she in the bakery judging for the show, but she was looking after the farmyard nursery. She hung the phone up thoughtfully. Between the show, work, and a trip to Melbourne, she should manage to keep out of Liam's way until he left. It was only four weeks till Christmas, and he said he would be leaving before then. Maybe she could get through this with her heart intact. She picked up a pen and wrote independence, confidence, and determination on a piece of paper next to the phone. She tore it off, folded it in half, and placed it in her pocket. All she had to do now was get her head to convince her heart to follow suit.

Chapter Eleven

'The spiel that the company is giving out to the media is a smokescreen.' Liam stood at the front of the auditorium in Prickle Creek R.S.L. Club and pointed to the PowerPoint that he had put together over the weekend. He'd talked to Jim Ison and made some calls to his journalist mates in the newspapers in Sydney. 'Even the figures they quote from the other mines can be proven incorrect by just looking at the production figures at the other sites.'

The crowd murmured, and Jim Ison stood up. 'They've underestimated this community. They've dismissed us as a bunch of uninformed cowboys, and I vote that we put up a decent fight. Other communities have taken them on and won. We can do it here. What do you all think?'

Heads nodded around the almost full room, and Liam looked to the back of the auditorium as an unfamiliar man stood to speak.

'For those of you who don't know me, I'm Clive Barker. My farm is at the northern point of the Western Way. Last week, I had a couple of blokes come knocking on my back door to tell me they would be laying a pipe right through my property. I told them to bugger off.'

There was a movement at the door, and Liam glanced across. Angie was standing at the back of the room near the main entrance. Clive's voice faded into the background, and for a moment, Liam lost focus. He cleared his throat as he looked away. He hadn't seen her for a few days, but she had been constantly in his thoughts. No matter what he was doing, she kept popping into his mind.

'So I suggest you all padlock your front gates.' Clive folded his arms and leaned against the door as the crowd murmured in assent. Liam's head lifted as Jim took the microphone again.

'I'd like to nominate Liam Smythe to be the official spokesperson for the Prickle Creek Alliance. Who's with me?'

Jim Ison looked at the assembled group. 'Is there anyone else who would like to nominate themselves or someone else?' No one put forward another nomination, and Jim turned to Liam. 'Do you accept the nomination?'

Liam stared at the back of the room, where Angie was still leaning against the wall. If he accepted this role, it would mean he would have to stay in town for the rest of this year and maybe a couple of months into next year. He thought quickly; the job in Sydney was being interviewed soon. If he was successful—and the word was, the job was his—the interview was just a formality, and the starting date would still be negotiable. One thing he'd learned over the past few weeks was that the farm was too big for one person to manage easily. If he stayed over Christmas, he could help Sebastian when he arrived to take over for this turn. No one knew how long Gran and Pop were going to be away. Liam had a feeling that the grandparents were testing them out to see if any of them fell in love with the place and wanted to take it over on a permanent basis. Thoughts flew through his mind as he processed the pluses and minuses of staying for a few weeks longer. He could afford to stay until just after the New Year and then head to the city. If he got the ABC job; if not, he'd have to look further afield.

Liam turned to Jim and held out his hand. 'I'd be honoured to accept the position, Jim.'

He'd think about what that meant for his career path later. The applause was heartening and filled him with confidence. He looked to the back of the auditorium, but Angie had gone.

***

So, how am I supposed to deal with this turn of events?

Angie bit her lip as she walked from the RSL club towards the milk bar. Her whole strategy of coping with Liam being here had been dependent on him only being around for a few more weeks as he'd said. If he took on the role on the alliance committee—and he had—he was probably going to be around for a while longer.

Angie was due to meet Lucy at the milk bar for coffee to discuss the upcoming agricultural show, and she tried to push aside her anxiety. She had to get on with her life and make a place for herself in this town. Helping out at the show and the ball would give her the opportunity to meet some other locals she hadn't met through her vet practice. She quickly processed a new plan. If there was one thing she had in bucketloads, it was resilience. She'd quickly learned to cope with what life threw at her when her father had left and her mother had died. The next few months would pass quickly. She would keep herself busy at work, keep a low profile in town—as much as she could with all these committees, shows, and balls—and avoid seeing Liam.

She pulled out a chair at one of the small wooden tables outside the milk bar and waited for Lucy. It wasn't long before a dust-covered ute pulled up, and Lucy bounced out of the driver's door. She hurried around to the other side and lifted out a pram, and a minute or two later, she had James safely ensconced in the pram and was pushing it across to Angie.

Angie smothered a smile. In her work clothes, she felt colourless next to Lucy. Jeans and a plain T-shirt were sensible clothes beneath her lab coat when dealing with animals all day. Lucy was wearing a pair of bright yellow tights with black spots and a matching yellow T-shirt.

She had never met anyone with the energy and enthusiasm that Lucy had. She seemed to throw herself into everything she did at full speed. Angie had been surprised to hear from Cissy that

Lucy had only recently moved back to the Pilliga Scrub from the city. She'd thought Lucy was a long-term local.

'Hi Angie.' Her voice was as bright as her clothes, and Angie made the effort to sit up straight and look happier.

'Hi Lucy, how's young James?' She peered into the pram. The cute baby boy was sound asleep, his little lips pursed in a bow. 'Oh look, he's grown already.'

'He has.' Lucy pulled out the other chair and sat back with a sigh. 'It's so good to be out and about. Garth and Liam have been treating me like an invalid. Honestly, they've been driving me crazy. Overprotective.' She looked at Angie, and a frown crossed her brow. 'I hope this isn't rude to say, but you look really tired. Are you okay?'

'I'm fine.' Angie summoned a smile. 'Just extra busy at work.'

Lucy leaned over and touched Angie's hand. 'Well, don't overdo it. We need you to be bright and fresh for the show. I was so pleased to hear from Sally that you're on board. They need some young ideas for the next show. And now they've got the two of us.' Her smile was wide. 'It's so good to have you in town. I'd love to introduce you to some of the girls I went to school with. I've been re-establishing friendships since I moved back. Prickle Creek is a great place to live.' Lucy laughed and shook her head. 'I never thought I'd say that. I thought I was a city girl.'

'What changed your mind?' Angie tipped her head to the side.

'Garth.' A sweet smile spread over Lucy's face. 'We were an item at high school, but we both moved away. I came back when Pop had his knee operation, and I fell in love. It's a story to hear over a glass of wine one night.'

'I look forward to it.' Angie looked up as Con, the milk bar owner, came out with an order pad.

'What'll it be, ladies?'

After they'd ordered a coffee for Angie and a malted milkshake for Lucy, Lucy turned back to Angie. 'Now, tell me all about you. Where you grew up, why you chose the Pilliga and all about living in London. I am so jealous of that,' she babbled on as Angie looked at her in surprise. 'I guess I'll—'

Angie widened her eyes. *Lucy knew she'd lived in London.*

'Oh.' Lucy stopped in mid-sentence. 'You look surprised. Liam told me you lived in London. And look, if we are going to be friends, I need to be honest with you. I do know,' she lowered her voice, 'that you and Liam were together for a while.'

Angie put down the coffee mug and took a deep breath. Before she could speak, Lucy continued. 'But now tell me all about your fiancé. Liam told me you're engaged now?' She glanced down at Angie's left hand. 'You don't wear your ring to work?'

'I didn't realise I'd be the subject of conversation.' Angie's voice shook, and she felt bad when Lucy's expression clouded. She hadn't meant to sound short with her.

'I'm sorry. I didn't mean to be nosy.' Lucy cleared her throat and then waited as Con put their drinks on the table. 'Liam and I are really close. He mentioned your name to me. It was a while back when he was giving me some good advice when I was moving back to the city. He was upset when I put two and two together. I won't say anything. Even Garth doesn't know.'

'Two and two?' Angie asked slowly. Lucy was moving too fast for her. 'When?'

Lucy waved her hand. 'I recognised your name when you called in last week, and Liam introduced you. Liam hadn't said a word, so don't think badly of him. He's a sweetie, even though we do fight.' She reached for her milkshake and sipped it. 'Now tell me all about this new man of yours. He must be pretty good if you picked him over Liam.' She smiled apologetically. 'I can say that because he is my cousin, and I do love him.'

Angie opened her mouth and then closed it. She reached for her coffee as she wondered what to say. Lucy was not a part of this. It was unfair to lie to her.

Why had life suddenly become so complicated? All she'd wanted was to come to this part of the outback, have her practice, and live happily. Tears pricked at her eyes and Angie put her coffee cup down before she dug in her pocket for a tissue. Her fingers closed over the piece of paper she'd put there earlier, and she bit her lip. *Confidence and independence.* She'd stood in front of the fridge this morning and repeated the words over and over, but the affirmation hadn't worked yet. It was going to take a few days—or weeks. And now that Liam was part of the alliance, it could be months. So, add determination to the mix.

'Angie, what's wrong? Are you okay?' Lucy's voice was full of concern.

Angie dabbed at her eyes. 'You are going to think very badly of me, and I really hoped we could be friends.' She meant it. Lucy had a lightness about her and a sense of fun, and that was just what Angie needed.

'Why, what's wrong? Come on, it can't be that bad.' Lucy put her milkshake down, reached over, and took Angie's hand. 'Come on, you can tell Aunty Lucy.'

'I know you're Liam's cousin, and your first loyalty is to him, but I can't lie to you. If I ask you to keep something to yourself, will you? I need to tell Liam myself.'

Lucy squeezed her hand. 'Of course, I will. Anything that upsets you so much stays between us. Even if you've broken the law. As long as it's not murder.' She smiled, and Angie knew it was an attempt to cheer her up and give her confidence. 'I probably can't condone that.'

She groaned and then shook her head. 'It's nothing as bad as that. I let Liam keep thinking something that's not true. He made an assumption, and I've let him keep thinking that. Now it's got complicated, and I have to tell him, but I don't want to because he might think I'm telling him I want him still.' The words came out in a rush and she sat back with a sigh.

'Whoa, slow down.' Lucy leaned forward. 'This sounds complicated. You can trust me not to spill, girlfriend. It will be our secret.'

'Okay,' she said slowly. 'So Liam told you there's a new man in my life?'

'Yes, he did,' she said slowly. 'And now that we're being truthful with each other, I can tell you he wasn't very happy about it. Grant someone?'

Angie chuckled, relief flooding through her when she knew she could trust Lucy with the truth. 'That's the first problem. I can never remember his name. Greg, Gary, Hugh, Grant. I even called him Garth once!'

'What do you mean? You can't remember his name?' Lucy stared at her. 'Why is that?'

'Hugh, the fiancé who Liam spoke to, is my friend's boyfriend.'

'What?' Lucy's voice was a squawk.

'Liam rang me one night when Hugh was visiting Jenny— we shared a house together in Melbourne. Hugh answered the phone, and they must have got their wires crossed when they were chatting. Hugh likes to have a yarn, and he would have been being friendly. Somehow, Liam assumed he was living there with me. I didn't even give it a thought because the last thing I expected was to run into Liam in outback New South Wales. The last time I saw him was in London, and I thought he'd stay there.' Now that she'd confessed, her words tumbled out over one another. 'He didn't want to come back to Australia with me.'

Lucy stared at her, her mouth open, but her eyes crinkled as her lips closed and tilted into a smile. 'Oh, Angie, I can see how that happened.'

'Every time I went to tell Liam, we'd get interrupted. And I keep calling him Grant and not Hugh because Liam and I used to joke about how much he hated Hugh Grant movies. It's just the silliest situation.'

Lucy burst out laughing, and Con, the milk bar proprietor, looked over at them with a smile.

Angie started laughing, too. 'So don't you say anything. I'll tell him. Soon.'

'Oh, sweetie. Trust me. I won't say a word. But I do know that it will keep Liam interested.'

'I don't want him interested. Because he's going again.'

'Getting Liam to stay here.'

'Oh, no.' Angie shook her head. 'Don't you go getting any ideas, Lucy! I just want the time to pass, keep myself busy, and survive until he moves back to the city.'

Lucy leaned back in her chair. 'You know what? I don't know that Liam will go back to the city. He's taken to farm life like a duck to water. I think it's in our blood.'

'Oh no! He has to. If he stays here, I'll have to leave. And I can't afford to do that. I've put all of my savings into the practice, and I've taken out a big loan. I've made a commitment, and I have to wait him out.'

James started to fret, a soft little cry coming from the pram. Lucy reached in and lifted the baby to her shoulder, gently patting his back. 'Can I ask you something personal? I know we don't know each other well, but I think we are going to be great friends.'

'Sharing a secret like that makes for a good friendship beginning.' Angie smiled. She couldn't help but like Lucy, even though she was related to Liam. She was friendly, open, honest and full of fun. 'Okay, fire away. But I may not answer.'

'If there is one thing I am, it's direct. If I'm going to help you get through this, I need to know one thing. Two things, actually.'

'Yes?' Angie's voice was soft as she waited.

'Why did you make up Gary?'

Angie giggled. *'Grant.'*

Lucy chuckled with her. 'Okay, *Grant.* Why did you need to make up a fiancé? Even when you thought Liam wasn't going to come back to Australia?'

Angie stared past her to the main street. The produce store building across the road was tired, and the paint was peeling from the sign that said Cartwright's Farm Produce. The museum next to the store was open, but no tourists were wandering through. The town was quiet, and a pang of something unfamiliar shot through Angie. She felt at home here, and she'd like to be a part of Prickle Creek and help build it up into a thriving community. She turned back to Lucy, who was watching her intently. 'Honestly?'

Lucy nodded.

'It was a spur-of-the-moment thing, one night a few months after I came back home. Liam and I had stayed in touch by email. And,' she shrugged, 'I was missing him like crazy. I knew I couldn't go on like that. I was looking at buying the practice here in Prickle Creek, and I knew I had to make a break. The most permanent way to end it was to tell him I'd met someone else.'

'What did Liam have to say about that?'

'Not a lot. When I left London, it was funny. He seemed happy enough to see me leave, and we didn't talk about a long-distance relationship. I left, not knowing if we were still a couple or if my leaving was the end of us. Or even if there was an "us".'

Lucy shook her head. 'Of course, there was. You were

living together, weren't you?'

'We never said or did anything about ending whatever we had. It just fizzled out when I left.' Angie bit her lip, thinking back to the tears she'd shed on the plane on the long flight home. 'I found it so hard.' She took a deep breath, but her voice still shook with the emotion she was clamping down. 'God, Lucy, I was so damn lonely without him, and in his emails to me, his life seemed to be going on as normal. I don't think he even noticed I was gone. So I sent a few emails over a couple of months, saying I was going out to the movies or dinner. I introduced him to the idea of me seeing someone slowly; I mean, I couldn't come up with an instant fiancé, could I?'

'And what did he say?'

'He didn't even comment about it.'

'He wouldn't have believed an instant fiancé, I suppose.' Lucy looked at her thoughtfully. 'Liam has never been one to talk about how he feels, you know.'

Angie nodded. 'I know, but after another six months passed, and Liam kept emailing me as though nothing was different, I rang him in London one night to tell him I was getting engaged, that Grant had asked me to marry him. Honestly, Lucy, it was the only way I could move on. It was the only way to cut all ties.' Finally, her voice shook. 'It was the *only* way to keep my self-esteem.' She didn't tell Lucy that she had cried all night after hearing his voice. If only she'd had the confidence to ask Liam what he really thought, what he intended, maybe things would have been easier, but Angie had lacked that confidence.

Lucy reached out with her free hand and patted Angie's arm. 'You poor thing. Men are so thoughtless sometimes. They just don't get it, do they?'

'Nope.' Angie sat up straight. 'Anyway, you know all about me now, warts and all. So what I have to do is keep busy and wait for Liam to leave.' She held Lucy's gaze. 'Because you're wrong, you know. Liam will leave. He's too immersed in his career and his causes to stay here in the outback.'

Lucy shook her head slowly. 'Maybe there's something here to keep him at home on Prickle Farm.'

'This new alliance thing he's got involved with.'

Lucy frowned. 'Alliance?'

'Liam agreed to take on the role of spokesperson for the alliance this morning at the meeting over at the RSL club.'

'I didn't know, but that's fantastic. It just reinforces that he will stay. The outback and the love for the land are in our blood, and Liam is just now beginning to realise that.' Lucy leaned forward and put the now-sleeping baby back in the pram. 'Now, for my second question.'

Angie had a feeling she wasn't going to like this one.

'Do you still love Liam?'

She took another deep breath and nodded slowly. 'I do. But there's no future in it. And that's why there is an imaginary Grant. He's my protection from a totally broken heart.'

Lucy's nod was brisk this time. 'I understand. And don't worry, any time you want to talk, you give me a call. Now we'd better talk about this show. Has Sally talked about the roster to you?'

Angie was surprised by Lucy's easy acceptance of her answer and the sudden switch of topic.

Surprised and a little unsettled.

Chapter Twelve

Liam spent the rest of the week at the farm. He'd delivered the cake safely to the show, pleased that the entry was in Lucy's name. Not that it was unmanly to bake a cake, but he had a reputation to uphold. He could just imagine the laughter of the boys in the newsroom back in London. If they ever got wind that he'd baked a cake to enter in an outback agricultural show, they'd about fall over laughing. He smiled. Not that he'd done much of the cake baking once Angie had turned up. He deliberately pushed her out of his thoughts. He wasn't going there. He wouldn't be here for much longer; she had a new man, so no matter how much he was still attracted to her, he would resist spending too much time in her company.

He'd really stuffed up that night in London when she'd come home and told him she was leaving. That she had to leave. But she hadn't asked him what he thought about it. Angie had just briskly set about making the arrangements and getting herself packed. It was as though she couldn't wait to leave him behind. And getting engaged to another man within a few months of coming home showed that she hadn't cared about him as much as he had loved her.

Yep, he'd loved her. But he'd never got around to telling her, and just as well. He would have looked like a fool. A bloody fool. He'd had a near miss there.

Liam reached down and scratched Willow's chin. It was late Thursday night, and he was sitting at the desk in the farm office. Whenever he sat there, the little pup curled up on his feet and kept him company. He'd spent the past few nights researching the Christos Company that was behind the gas exploration. Now that Jim Ison had sent over the information, Liam had discovered some disturbing details, and he was drafting an introductory article for the city papers. Just to see what response it got from the company. He'd found that putting the issue out there often got to the truth of the matter.

Shame he hadn't applied that to his personal life. He shook his head. It was time to focus on his work. Put Angie Edmonds out of his mind.

The cattle work had kept him busy since Garth had come over on Sunday and helped him catch up on the drenching. Lucy came with him and sat on the fence, just like when they were kids. This time, she had little James strapped to her chest in one of those sling things. When they'd finished, she'd put James to bed in his pram and made them a cup of tea. They'd sat on the verandah, and she'd been full of questions.

'I hear you've joined the alliance,' she'd said.

'Yeah, I'll do my bit for the area while I'm here.' Liam had wiped his hand over his brow. Spring was passing quickly, and summer was just around the corner.

'So, what's the plan?' Lucy passed over one of the scones she'd brought over. Liam wolfed it down and held his hand out for another one.

'What plan?'

Lucy waved her hand. 'Sebastian, Jemima, you? When are they coming home? And are you going back to Sydney like you'd planned?' Her eyes narrowed as she waited for his response.

'Seb and Jemmy will be home at the beginning of December. We'll overlap for a couple of weeks, maybe a few more, and then I'll be off. What's with the sudden interest? Nothing's changed.'

'Yes, it has.' Her smile was sweet, and Liam frowned.

'No, it hasn't.'

Garth rolled his eyes. 'You pair!'

'You're the spokesperson for the alliance now. You can't take on a role like that and then hare straight back to Sydney.' Lucy folded her arms. 'Besides, you'll have to be here for James's christening, anyway.'

'I can still work in Sydney and come back here.'

'Why would you?' This time, Lucy rolled her eyes.

'Why would I what?'

'Work in Sydney. Why wouldn't you stay here? With your finger on the pulse, you know.'

Liam narrowed his eyes. 'Why the sudden interest in my plans?'

'Because I need to know about Christmas Day. "Maybe" isn't good enough. Everyone will be home, and I think you should be here, too. The first family Christmas we've all had together for a long time. Garth's parents are flying up from the south coast, and I would love you to be here. And I was wondering how you would cope with being away if you're working on the alliance, too.' Lucy waved a hand casually. 'Anyway, what time are you going to the show tomorrow? Do you want a lift in with us so you can have a celebratory drink when you win the blue ribbon for Gran's cake?'

'Whoa, there.' Liam put his hand up. 'I won't win the blue ribbon. The entry's in your name.'

Lucy smiled. 'But you baked the cake. And you deserve to celebrate.'

'I wasn't going to go to the show. I've got too much going on here.'

'What! Not go to the show? You have to. Everyone goes to the show.'

Garth nodded. 'I'm with Luce on that one, Liam. You have to come, mate. It's one of the high points of the year for the district.'

'And I've offered to drive us in so you can have a couple of drinks and relax in the beer tent.' Lucy giggled. 'You have to be there for the cake judging, anyway. Apparently, it's a family tradition.' Innocence filled her expression. 'And Angie's on the judging panel.'

Liam came in from the paddocks late on Friday morning, showered, and dug out some decent jeans and a clean T-shirt. It would be the first time he'd been off the farm in more than a week. There'd been plenty of work to keep him busy, but the main reason he'd avoided going to town was to stay away from Angie. That was something he'd have to deal with if he ran into her today, and it was very likely that he would. Prickle Creek wasn't that big, although he remembered the agricultural show as a well-attended event when he was in his teens. He'd stay away from her. There was no need to feed this attraction that was still there. He'd dreamed about her the last couple of nights. He frowned as he ran a comb through his hair in front of the bathroom mirror.

Who am I kidding? It was hard to stay away from her. He shrugged and threw the comb down on the dresser. A horn beeped, and he picked up his Akubra hat and a jacket. It might be a late night.

Liam smiled as he climbed into the front of the SUV with Lucy. Garth was sitting in the back seat with James in his baby capsule, and a multitude of bags and picnic baskets almost obscured his view.

'Are we going for the whole weekend?' he asked with a laugh.

'It's alright for you, mate,' Garth grumbled from the back seat. 'I'm a family man now.'

'And I get to drive because James is about to wake up and cry, and it's Garth's turn to look after him. I was up half the night.'

And cry, the baby did, all the way to town. By the time they pulled into the showground on the southern side of town, Liam was pleased to be out of the car. Who'd have thought that such a small human being could make so much noise?

'I might cadge a lift back to the farm with someone else later,' he said with a grin, rubbing his ears.

'Get away with you. You'll be a dad one day.' Lucy nudged him as he helped unload the ute.

'I can't see that happening.' Liam helped Garth with the baskets and boxes, but there were still too many to carry.

'Leave those ones there until we eat later.' Lucy pointed at the coolers.

'I can't understand why you brought all that food. I would have been happy with a Dagwood Dog,' Liam said, and Garth nodded.

'We have a healthy picnic to eat later,' Lucy said.

The parking area for the show took up three paddocks of the farm adjacent to the showground. A continuous line of cars, trucks and utes—and even the occasional large bus—turned onto the grassy paddock as he watched. Liam smiled as he lifted his head. The smell of hot dogs and doughnuts filled the air, and the tinkling music from the merry-go-round echoed around him. Children whooped and screamed as the Zipper dipped and lifted into the air, and he remembered the great fun he and his three cousins had had every year at the show when they'd been small children…and teenagers. It was something he'd forgotten, living away from the outback. The annual show was a chance to show your animals and produce and hang out with your friends. It was the high point of the Prickle Creek social calendar.

He followed Garth and Lucy through the gates and nodded at Jim Ison as he paid for his ticket.

'How's the article going, Liam?' Jim passed him the programme for the weekend.

'Almost done, Jim. If you've got some free time today, it would be good to sit and have a chat. I've uncovered quite a bit about Christos, and I'd like to find out how much you already know.'

'How about meeting in the beer tent after the cattle judging? I'll be ready for a beer after that.'

'Sounds good,' Liam said.

Jim smiled. 'Did you enter any cattle this year?'

'No, that was my grandfather's area.'

'So you'll be spending most of your time in the pavilion waiting to hear about your cake?' Jim tipped his hat at Liam with a broad smile.

'My cake?' Liam looked around suspiciously, but Lucy had disappeared.

As he turned, his mouth dried, and his heart picked up a beat. Angie was walking out of the main pavilion. A brightly coloured dress just brushed her knees, and her hair was loose and blowing in the slight breeze. A huge smile wreathed her face as she caught sight of Lucy. Liam narrowed his eyes as the two women greeted each other with a hug and put their heads together in conversation.

When did that happen? Lucy hadn't mentioned that she'd palled up with Angie. He swallowed as suspicion flooded through him. He knew his cousin all too well, and a couple of things she'd said on Sunday began to make sense. She'd been full of questions, and Liam suspected that Lucy was on a matchmaking bent.

God, that was the last thing he needed. He was going back to Sydney, and Angie was staying here.

He'd be pulling Lucy aside and having a little cousinly chat to tell her to pull her head in the first opportunity he got. He'd also have to warn Angie that once Lucy got an idea in her mind, it was hard to move her on.

Liam lifted his hat, nodded, and turned away as Angie looked away from Lucy and caught him staring.

'Liam.'

He turned as Garth called him.

'Can you mind James and the bags for a minute? I need to stow all this gear that Lucy's packed somewhere.'

'Sure. It'll give me a chance to read the programme.' Liam laughed. 'Everything but the kitchen sink is there by the look of things. You were pretty cramped in the back of the car.'

Garth walked off towards the main office beside the gate, and Liam looked down and checked on James before he pulled the show programme from his pocket. As he read down the list of events, a sweet jasmine smell surrounded him, and he looked up slowly, knowing who was standing beside him, before his gaze settled on Angie. He'd recognise that perfume anywhere. Hell, it had even been in his dreams this past week.

'Hi, Liam.' Her voice was sweet and soft, and he ignored the warm feeling that filled his chest as she spoke.

'Hello, Ange, sorry, I mean, Angie.' God, he was stammering like a teenage boy, the teenage boy he'd been the last time he'd attended the Prickle Creek Agricultural Show. 'You look lovely.'

A rose-coloured blush ran up her neck and her cheeks, and a measure of satisfaction flitted through Liam. She wasn't as immune to him as she tried to make out. But if he was fair, they'd lived together for almost two years and knew each other very well.

Very well.

'Thank you. Lucy asked me to come over and tell you she had to go and see someone.'

'Someone?'

Angie lifted her shoulders in a soft shrug, and the shoulder of her dress slipped off, revealing creamy, smooth skin. Liam resisted the urge to run the back of his hand over skin that he knew would be soft to his touch.

Her blush deepened as she tugged her dress up. 'Yes, she said she won't be long.' She cleared her throat. 'Are you going to watch the cake judging?'

'Maybe.'

This time, she smiled. 'You know I'm presenting the awards? I tried to tell Sally that I was at Prickle Creek Farm when you baked your entry, but she said as long as it's not entered in my name, that's fine.'

'It's Lucy's entry,' Liam said.

Angie frowned and shook her head. 'No, I saw the cake on the stand in the pavilion. It definitely says Liam Smythe, Prickle Creek Farm.'

'Jeez, you must be joking!' Liam ran his hand through his too-long hair. He really was overdue for a haircut. 'Wait until I see Lucy. She must have switched it over. Honestly, she is a minx.'

Angie leaned over and peered into the pram. James was sound asleep. 'You're doing a great job babysitting, so I'm sure no one will have a problem with you baking a cake.' When she looked back up at him, her expression was innocent, but her eyes were dancing. Liam couldn't help smiling. 'Although,' she said, 'I must warn you, you are the only male entrant.'

Liam groaned. 'All my credibility has flown out the window.'

'Don't be sexist.' Angie pointed to the pavilion. 'Have a look at who won the blue ribbon for needlework.'

'Who?'

'Go and see. Look, here comes Garth, and then you should come in to hear the cake winners.' Angie wiggled her fingers in a cute little wave as she walked away. 'I'll see you in there, okay?'

'Thanks, mate.' Garth took the pram handle from Liam as

he stared after Angie. 'We can put the picnic baskets and a couple of the bags behind the counter.'

'I'll give you a hand.' Liam picked up the bags and followed Garth into the building.

'I don't know where Lucy's disappeared to,' Garth said.

'Probably avoiding me.' Liam shook his head. 'She entered the bloody cake in my name.'

Garth choked back a laugh. 'Nothing wrong with that.'

'I know. I've already been accused of being sexist.'

They stowed the bags safely, and Garth turned to Liam with a grin. 'You head into the cake judging, and I'll head over to the ring to watch the cattle judging. I'll meet you for a cup of tea later.' Garth crooked his little finger and snorted.

'You'll keep, mate. I'll see you in the beer tent later.' He swaggered off and turned to Garth, and his grin was as wide as his cousin-in-law's. 'Now, I'm going to go win me a blue ribbon in the cake baking. Gotta keep Gran's record intact.'

As Liam walked into the pavilion, the smells of fresh produce surrounded him. The wall at the far end was decorated in the shape of the Pilliga region. Oranges, limes, and apples provided a colourful display. A huge sheep had been fashioned out of wool on a stand, situated proudly in front of the needlework entries. Liam couldn't help wandering over and looking at the needlework entries. In pride of place sat a handmade quilt, and as he leaned over to see who had won the prize, a deep booming voice came from behind him.

'Well, if it isn't young Liam Smythe!'

He turned and stood face to face with Gordon MacArthur, the headmaster of the high school he'd attended in Prickle Creek. Well, he had been headmaster when Liam had left school ten years ago. 'Mr MacArthur. Good to see you.' Liam held his hand out, and the older man took it.

'Gordon, please. You're not in my office anymore.' He shook Liam's hand with a firm grip. 'I wondered if it was you when I saw the name on the big chocolate cake. I don't remember you studying home science when you were at school.'

Liam stifled a groan. 'No, I didn't. I've entered on my grandmother's behalf. They're away on a trip to New Zealand.'

'Yes, I heard you've moved back to the Pilliga.'

Liam didn't correct him. 'Anyway, it's good to see you back and entering into the community spirit. Good luck in the judging.' As the headmaster walked away, Liam leaned forward, and this time he smiled.

First prize in needlework: Gordon MacArthur.

If it was good enough for his headmaster, it was good enough for him. He made his way confidently to the end of the pavilion, where rows of cakes, scones, and slices were arranged on a long table with three tiers. At the end, a large refrigerated cabinet was filled with a display of frosted cakes; a group of women stood beside the stand, each with a clipboard and pencil in hand. On the top shelf was his chocolate cake, and it didn't look too bad, if he did say so himself. From where he was, he couldn't see if there were ribbons on the cakes.

Liam stood back as the group of judges moved on and waited until he got a good view of Angie. She looked at home, smiling and chatting with the other women as they discussed each entry and awarded a score before moving on to the next entry. He took a deep breath as confusion filled him. His feelings for Angie hadn't changed. He knew that the year or so since she'd left him in London had been empty, and he hadn't been happy. A part of him had left with her, and he'd buried himself in his work. He'd never forget the frustration that had consumed him the night she had called him. Hearing her voice had been wonderful until she'd told him she'd chosen another man to spend her life with.

He clenched his fists by his side. He was being a bloody dog in the manger. Angie deserved happiness. Even though she'd never said much about it, apart from talking about the grief of when her mother had died, he knew she'd had a tough childhood. It was good that she'd found a man to love her, a man who was prepared to marry and spend his life with her.

It was.

The crackling of the microphone interrupted his thoughts, and he turned to the stage.

'Testing, one, two, three.' An older woman stood on the stage, tapping the microphone.

Liam looked around. Angie was standing at the bottom of the steps leading up to the small stage and presentation area. As he looked across, her gaze was on him, and colour flooded her cheeks as she quickly looked away. He'd caught her looking at him; that was interesting. That was the second time he'd caught her eyes on him. He must make her feel awkward. It was time they had a bit of a talk to clear the air. Things had been left unresolved when she'd left him in London—no, scrub that—when he'd let her leave without him. If he was honest, it was the biggest regret of his life, and now it was too late to do anything about it. She was living here, and he would move on. Again.

Forget talking about it; all he had to do was avoid her, like he'd planned. He shouldn't have come to the damned show. He'd let Lucy talk him into it way too easily.

He took a step back and leaned against one of the few pieces of wall that wasn't covered with posters or entries. He'd wait until the winners were announced unless Lucy made an appearance, and then he'd head over to the cattle show and leave her to it.

Ten minutes later, Liam was filled with impatience. He shifted from one foot to the other. How many damn categories of cakes and scones could there be? And to make it worse, every time the category changed, they switched over the judges on the microphone announcing the winners. He lifted his head as a soft, familiar voice filled the pavilion.

Angie cleared her throat and gripped the microphone tightly. He remembered she'd never been confident in public situations. He closed his eyes, remembering the night they'd met. She'd been the quiet one in the corner, but he hadn't been able to take his eyes off her.

'It gives me great pleasure to announce the winners of the baking competition and, of course, announce the Cake-of-the-Show winner: the ultimate blue ribbon and a hundred-dollar voucher.' Her voice firmed, and Liam's attention focused on the judging.

Angie announced each of the winners of the various categories, and each person climbed the steps and shook her hand before she handed each woman—yep, all women, not another man in sight, not even the headmaster—the prize voucher. Liam let his appreciative gaze linger. Angie was slightly built, but the dress hugged the curves she had in all the right places. Her skin was fair, and her hair fell softly onto her shoulders. She was the prettiest woman in the whole pavilion, and his gut clenched. He couldn't wait to get back to the city; it would be easier there to get her out of his head.

The speakers emitted a high-pitched whistle, and Angie held the microphone away for a moment. Liam could have sworn he saw a smile in her eyes as she glanced across at him. 'Now we move to the Cake-of-the-Show section. As you all know, I am new to the district, but I've been told that the winner of this ribbon has won it for fifty years in a row. What a record! Helena Peterkin, from Prickle Creek Farm, who is taking a well-earned rest away with her husband, I believe.'

Liam shuffled his feet. In a way, he didn't want to win, but it was probably important to Gran that the farm kept their winning streak intact. And the cake had turned out pretty well with Angie and Lucy's help.

Her voice got louder. 'The winner of the blue ribbon for this year is … Liam Smythe, on behalf of Prickle Creek Farm.'

A round of applause surrounded Liam as he pushed himself away from the wall and headed self-consciously for the stage where Angie waited, clutching the last prize voucher of the day. He took the six steps two at a time. The sooner this was over and done with, the better. As he stopped in front of Angie, the gleam of an idea came into his head. He let a lazy grin spread over his face as he stood nonchalantly on the stage.

Damn being embarrassed. He won the prize for Gran. Prickle Creek's reputation is upheld.

Angie held her hand out to him. 'Congratulations, Liam.'

Before she could read his intent, he took her hand and leaned forward, catching her lips in a kiss, much to the delight of the spectators. The applause grew louder, and a couple of whoops and whistles came from the back of the pavilion. He pulled back and took the ribbon and the prize voucher from Angie. Her cheeks were pink, and her lips were slightly parted. It was all he could do not to put his arms around her and kiss her again.

This time, she must have seen his intent, because even though she murmured softly, her voice was like steel. 'Don't even think about it.' Turning to the side away from him, she flicked the switch back on the microphone and made the closing announcement.

'Thanks for coming today, folks. I believe next up is the judging over in the small animal nursery.' Angie put the microphone back up on the stand and switched it off. Liam waited until she was ready to walk off the stage and held his arm out. 'I'll help you down the steps, Angie.'

The look on her face was one of frustration rather than anger. 'I'm perfectly capable of walking down a few steps, Liam.' Her expression softened. 'I only judged the appearance of the cake. I didn't taste it.' For a moment, he didn't understand what she was saying, and then he remembered Gran's secret ingredient.

'Ah, I thought you might have had a taste and would be wobbly on the steps.' He held her gaze and couldn't look away. For a moment, he imagined that the look in Angie's eyes was longing, just like he was feeling, but she pursed her lips and stared at him as the expression left her face.

She looked…sad. 'No, and I didn't tell anyone what was in it. That secret stays in your family.'

'I'd like you to meet Gran and Pop when they come home.'

This time, her voice was devoid of any expression. 'I'm sure I will. Most probably after you've left, I would say.'

'Yes, most probably.' He shoved the voucher in his shirt pocket. 'Hey, can you do me a favour?'

Angie looked at him with her eyebrows raised. 'Maybe. Depends on what it is.'

'Promise not to laugh?'

'Promise.' He was pleased to see her lips twitching already.

'I want to go on the dodgem cars, but when I walked past them on the way here, there was no one over fifteen on them.'

Angie's smile was wide. 'Why not? Let's have some fun and celebrate your award-winning cake.'

Liam grabbed her hand and led her through the crowd to Sideshow Alley. They wound their way along the dusty path, past the stalls filled with tacky soft animals in garish colours, past the ghost train, and the Ferris wheel that was in the middle of a paddock. Liam joined the queue, unable to believe that Angie had agreed to join him so readily.

'Single car each or a double?' the show hawker asked.

'Two, please.' Angie's smile was innocent, and she held his eye as he paid for the tickets.

'What are you up to?'

'Me?'

'Yes, you. I know that look, Ange.'

'I bet I can beat you.'

'Is that a challenge?'

She lifted her chin, brushed her loose hair back with one hand, and grinned at him. 'No, it's a statement. I bet you can't hit me with your car.'

Excitement and anticipation flickered through Liam. If he didn't know better, he would have said that Angie was flirting with him. 'That's a challenge to me. No man likes to be shown up in the dodgems. What are we playing for?' He bumped her with his shoulder as they waited for the current circuit to end.

'Um, let me think.' She tilted her head to the side, and the tip of her tongue touched her top lip. 'How about the loser gets to go on the ghost train?' She shivered and made a scary noise. 'Woo… All alone.'

Liam laughed. It was great to see Angie loosening up. 'Is that the best thing you can come up with?'

She shook her head, and her hair brushed against his face. 'There's not a lot to pick from at a country show.'

'If I bump you with my car—and I will'—Liam knew his smile was smug—'you can shout me a battered sav and a beer. Knowing Lucy, she'll have salad sandwiches packed for the picnic tea.'

Angie held her hand out. 'And if you don't, you can go on the ghost train. In the dark. All by yourself.'

He shook her hand as the ride operator opened the gate. 'You've got a deal.'

Angie took off and jumped into the car at the back of the

group—a bright red car with a yellow and red post and a smiley face. As Liam looked around at what was left, a group of teenagers pushed past him, and the ride operator nudged him.

'Go for that one, mate.' His grin was wide, and he had a tooth missing. 'Looks a bit sad, but it manoeuvres better than the rest.' He pointed to a black car with the paint peeling off it.

Liam grinned back at him and jumped into the car. He belted up and waited until the operator turned the cars on. The whirr of the electric motor kicked in as he depressed the pedal with both eyes firmly on his target. Round and round the circular track they went. Every time Angie got closer, Liam pushed the pedal down and wrenched the car in the opposite direction to her car, trying to get to the back to sneak up on her. The longer they played cat and mouse, the more determined he was to win. Screams of delight filled the small space as cars rammed into each other. The wheels rumbled on the timber floor, and the electricity crackled as the whip dragged across the roof. A kid yelled from the car in front of him as the car stopped dead, and Liam wrenched the wheel to the left to miss it. He took his eyes off Angie for a second, and when the car lurched forward again, he looked up, but her car was gone. He twisted his head to the left, but she wasn't there.

An excited squeal reached him, and at the same instant, a car slammed into the rubber at the back of his car.

'Winner, winner, chicken dinner.' Angie's triumphant yell rose above the rumbling noise.

Liam turned around, and she gave him a thumbs up; her laugh was wonderful to hear. It was worth losing just to hear that. The cars came to a stop, and they climbed out. Angie walked over with a wide smile.

'Ghost train now.'

He grabbed her hand and pulled her out of the enclosure and up to the building that the train was in. 'I'll do you a deal. You come with me, and I'll shout you a battered sav and a beer.'

She batted her eyelids at him. 'Oh, how can I resist an offer like that?'

They waited at the booth for the operator to appear. Gruesome noises and screams came from the building, and Liam caught her eye. Angie's face was flushed with a rosy glow, and she looked really happy. He glanced down at her hand. At least she wasn't wearing a ring.

Liam paid for their tickets, and they climbed into one of the train's small wagons. As it pulled into the darkness, a huge white figure swooped in front of them, and god damn it if he didn't jump a mile. Angie cackled, and her body shook with laughter.

'It wasn't that funny,' he said. 'I didn't get a fright. It was because we went over a bump.'

'Sure it was.' Her giggles lasted for the whole circuit, and when they came back into the light, her eyes were bright with laughter. 'Do you want to go again, or are you too scared?'

'No, I need to eat,' he said, his lips twitching.

'Thank you. That was fun.' Angie grabbed his hand. 'And the battered savs are my shout.'

Liam waited at the back of the queue as Angie stood near the caravan that was selling all manner of greasy but great-smelling food. After a few minutes, she turned and walked towards him, holding two huge battered saveloys on long sticks. As she approached, Liam caught sight of Lucy heading their way, pushing the pram. He grabbed Angie's arm. 'Quick, straight to the beer tent. We're about to get sprung.'

They pushed through the crowd and found a spare table in the back corner near the path that led to the pavilion. The tent was almost full, and the conversations washed around Liam as he went to the bar and came back with two cans of beer.

They sat together, content to watch the crowd walk past as

they ate.

Finally, Angie wiped her mouth with the napkin. 'That was disgustingly good.'

'It was. You want another one?'

'Oh no.' She held up her hand and covered her mouth. 'I'm done.'

Liam leaned back on the plastic chair and took a drink of the beer. The cold liquid soothed his parched throat.

'You really have settled well into outback life, haven't you, Angie?'

'Yes. I love it here in the Pilliga Scrub.' She lifted her chin as she spoke as if challenging him to dispute it. 'And I'm staying.'

'So do you reckon Hugh will come and live out here with you one day?'

'Hugh?' When her brow wrinkled in a frown, Liam was sorry he'd brought it up. The happy, comfortable mood fizzled in an instant.

'Hugh? You mean Grant?' she said.

Liam forced a laugh. 'Drat, if I don't get his name mixed up every time in my head. Hugh Grant. The actor always confuses me. Sorry, I mean Grant.'

'Look, Liam, it's not a problem because—'

Liam waved his hand. 'Don't worry, none of my business anyway. Look, here comes Lucy. She looks like a woman on a mission.'

'Hey, you pair,' Lucy called from outside the tent. 'I've been looking for you everywhere.' She looked at them curiously as she parked the pram beside the table. 'Everything okay?'

'Yes, all good. I walloped Liam in the dodge 'em cars.'

'And I lost on purpose so we could snuggle up in the dark in the ghost train.' This time, he dropped his voice suggestively. He couldn't help himself, and the look that Angie shot back as she stood was not pretty, although he was pleased to see that blush creeping up her cheeks.

'You did not! I beat you fair and square, so man up and admit it.' Angie glanced at her watch. 'Thanks for the beer, Liam. I'm going over to the animal nursery now. I'm helping supervise the kids.'

'Come on, I'm going there, too. Coming, Liam?' His cousin's voice was sweet, but the look on her face was far from it.

'No.' He knew his voice was gruff, but he didn't care. 'I'm staying here.' Why had he gone and ruined their fun with that stupid question about that bloke?

Chapter Thirteen

'I can't wait until James is old enough to feed the baby animals.'

Lucy stood beside Angie as they looked over at the children cuddling a variety of baby animals. Newly hatched chicks, baby lambs, and ducklings sliding down the waterslide provided a source of entertainment for the younger—and many older—showgoers.

'Don't wish him to grow up too quickly.' Angie stared out over the young children. The way she was going, she'd never have to worry about that.

'Come on, Angie, cheer up.' Lucy smiled at her. 'This is your first Prickle Creek show. Don't let Liam get you cranky. We've got the whole night ahead of us now that you've finished your judging. Besides, you've really got him rattled with this man of yours.'

'I was about to tell him the truth when you called us.' Angie forced a smile on her face, but she was miserable inside. The last thing she'd expected when she moved to Prickle Creek was to see Liam here or to have to deal with her feelings. 'Okay, I'm only on the roster here for half an hour. What treat have you got for me next?'

'Garth can take over James for a while, and I think we should do sideshow alley and win you some prizes. What do you say?' Lucy nudged Angie with her hip. 'Get that smile back on your face?'

This time, Angie's smile was genuine. 'I think that's just what I need. A bit of fun, some prizes and something sweet to eat. All I can taste is the grease from—' *Whoops. She almost slipped up.* Lucy had gone to so much trouble to pack a healthy picnic for them.

'From what?' Lucy frowned.

'Nothing. Come on, let's go win a soft toy for this young man.'

'Okay. You got it! I'll just go and leave James with Garth, and I'll meet you there in what, say, half an hour? Next to the dodge 'em cars.'

'See you there.'

Angie spent the next ten minutes extricating a small girl who'd got her foot caught in the duck waterslide and passing out brushes to a group of children who wanted to brush the coats of the baby donkeys. By the time she was relieved of her roster duty and headed to meet Lucy, her good mood was restored. There was no way she was going to let Liam upset her. They'd had such fun together on the cars and in the train and eating greasy food. If she was honest, he really hadn't done anything. Until he'd asked about Grant, she'd forgotten about Hugh, or Grant, Hugh Grant, or whoever.

She was just too damned sensitive. Confidence, she told herself. The time will go quickly. Once the show was over, she wouldn't have to see him again unless he came in with Willow.

Best laid plans and all that, she thought a while later when she and Lucy left the sideshow alley and headed for the fairy floss stall, carrying three stuffed animals that they had won.

'Ugh, I don't know how you can eat that stuff,' she said to Lucy.

'Lucy is renowned for her sweet tooth, aren't you, cuz?' Angie jumped when Liam appeared beside them as they walked along to the fairy floss stall.

'I love it. Makes me feel like a kid again.' Lucy smiled at them as she headed across to the food stall. Liam stood next to

Angie, and she focused on staying calm.

'Still enjoying sideshow alley, Ange?' He was standing a little too close to her, and she moved away a fraction.

'I am. I'm having fun.'

'So you're here to stay in the Pilliga?'

Angie took a deep breath and injected brightness into her voice. 'I am. Love the town, love the people, and love my work.'

Liam didn't reply, and a strange feeling ran through Angie. She would have loved the confidence to be honest and say what her heart was telling her. What she wanted to say.

It would be even better if I knew you were going to stay here too. But that wouldn't happen in a million years. *The Prickle Creek Chronicle*, the weekly local newspaper, wasn't quite the career move for a hot-shot journalist.

Lucy looked at them curiously as she rejoined them. 'So what now, guys?'

'I might head home,' Angie said. Being around Liam was too hard. She had to watch what she said, and he made her thoughts as cloudy as the fairy floss in the bag that Lucy was holding. The misunderstanding about Hugh was weighing her down, too. Would she ever get over these damn feelings for Liam?

'Oh, you can't leave. We've got a picnic dinner packed and a big enough rug for everyone to sit on while we watch the fireworks.'

'Fireworks?' Angie knew she was stuck here. Maybe there'd be an emergency call to the surgery or out to a farm a hundred kilometres away. She could hope for that.

But probably not. Everyone was at the show.

'Yes. There are two fireworks shows. One at eight so the littlies can go home, and then a bigger display at nine o'clock. Come on, stay and watch with us. I hope I wasn't assuming too much, but I brought enough dinner for you, too.'

Angie nodded. 'That's very kind of you to make me feel welcome. Of course, I'll stay.' She could have sworn that Liam let out his breath when she agreed. She must be very careful what she said tonight.

My fiancé's name is Grant, Grant!

'Oh Angie, I nearly forgot.' Lucy dug into her pocket and pulled out an envelope. 'An invitation for you to James's christening after Christmas. I meant to give you more notice in case you were going to go down to Melbourne in the holidays to visit—'

'Grant!' Angie filled in breathlessly.

'Yes, Grant.' Lucy smiled with a sideways glance at Liam, but he was watching the Zipper as the ride started up again. 'Maybe you could invite him, too.'

'Lucy.' Angie kept her voice low as she pulled a face and slipped the invitation into her pocket.

'Sorry,' Lucy whispered.

Liam turned back to them. 'So where's this sumptuous feast you've promised? I'm starving.' The breeze caught his hair, and Angie resisted the urge to reach up and brush it from his eyes. Once, she'd had the right to do that, but no more. Liam hadn't wanted her, and she had to get used to that. Being in his company was bringing back all of the old feelings. Even though he'd kissed her before—her lips were still tingling—she had no call to touch his hair.

'We brought most of it in, but there are two food coolers still in the car. I'll go over and collect Garth and James. Would you pair go over and get them out of the ute for me?' Lucy dug into her pocket and passed the keys to Liam.

'I can get them both. Angie, you go with Lucy.'

Relief flooded through Angie, and the last thing she wanted was to be alone with Liam again that night, especially since he seemed to be in a strange mood once he'd mentioned her fiancé.

'No, it'll take two of you. They're really heavy. Angie, you go with him.' Lucy nudged Angie.

Angie fought gritting her teeth. Really, Lucy was being way too obvious. She kept her voice impersonal. 'It's fine, Liam. I'll help. It's the least I can do, seeing as Lucy is feeding me, too.'

It was the last thing she wanted to do in the soft evening light—walk all the way through the showground to the car with Liam.

'Okay.' His deep voice sent a surge of warmth rushing through her.

The sun had set, and the lights of sideshow alley backlit the evening sky. The sky was painted in a palette of oranges, pinks and yellows, and the first star was peeking between the high clouds. The happy squeals of the children on the rides mixed with the raucous call of crows as they flapped in the darkening sky across the car park above them. Angie walked beside Liam as he led the way between the rows of cars. For a while the silence was awkward.

'There's much more interest in the show than when I was a kid,' he said.

'It's good to see so many people supporting the local community.'

Their conversation was stilted, and Angie put her hands in her pockets. The last time they'd walked together had been along the Embankment in London, and Liam had taken her up on the London Eye. She closed her eyes for a moment and took a breath as she remembered. She hated heights, and he'd convinced her she had to tick it off her bucket list. It had been a few weekends before she'd found out she had to go home.

He held her hand firmly in his as they negotiated the crowds across the Millennium pedestrian bridge along the Queen's Walk to the London Eye Pier. They stopped at the Doggetts Coat and Badge pub for a beer, and Liam held her hand at the table, rubbing his thumb over her skin. When they got into the passenger capsule, he held her even tighter because he knew how scared she was. When they reached the top, not worried about the others on the ride with them, he gently brushed her eyes closed with his fingertips and kissed her lips until she forgot she was more than a hundred metres above the Thames in a tiny metal capsule. He'd been gentle and kind in those days, and she'd loved him for his thoughtfulness.

Angie jumped as Liam stopped ahead of her and spoke. 'It's a bit like the London Eye, isn't it?'

God, is he a mind reader as well now?

'What is?' She kept her voice calm, even though her heart was racing from the memories of that kiss.

Liam pointed back to the sideshow alley, and she let her gaze follow his finger. The Ferris wheel was lit up as it moved slowly and ponderously in a circle. The colourful lights cast garish shadows on the tents of the sideshow alley where the showmen were hawking their rides.

Angie shivered, and Liam smiled down at her. 'Do you want a ride on the Ferris wheel?'

'No. I don't.'

'I thought the open buckets wouldn't appeal. What if I held your hand?'

'Liam.'

And then, damn him, he remembered, too. 'Or I could kiss you like I did on the London Eye.' His voice was soft, but his face was shadowed. 'What do you reckon, Ange?'

'Liam,' she repeated, and her voice was prim. 'What are you trying to do? Get me cranky? Tease me? Or what?'

'Hell, Angie. You want me to be honest?'

'I don't know.'

Liam turned away from her and ran his hand through his hair. 'I'll tell you one thing. I missed you when you left London.'

'You had no one to cook for you?' Angie's heart was thudding so hard, it was hurting. *Why is he doing this?*

'Don't be nasty. It doesn't suit you.'

'Well, stop trying to revisit the past. Those days are long gone. We've moved on, and we have to make the most of it. Being thrown together in this small town is… difficult.' She looked up at him as he turned to face her. 'It's awkward for both of us.'

'Yes, I'll admit it. It's hard, but it doesn't have to be, Angie.'

'Oh, yes, it does. What do you want to do? Take up where we left off? Forget about my fiancé'—her voice cracked—'and have a fling until you go back to Sydney, or your career, or London, wherever you end up? And leave me here to pick up the pieces again after you go?'

'Again?'

She waved her hand. 'You know what I mean.'

'No, I don't. What pieces?' He moved closer, and his voice was soft but deep and was almost her undoing.

'You'll move on, and I'll have the reputation of the woman who had a fling while her fiancé was away working. I have to live in this town. Surely, you remember what gossip mills country towns can be?'

'So, if it wasn't for the gossip, I could entice you?' Liam reached out and held her shoulders gently. Angie could feel her bottom lip begin to tremble. Being almost in Liam's arms was heaven and hell, all wrapped up into one.

She bit her lip to stop it shaking and looked up at him. 'Please don't, Liam. Don't do this to me.' She tried to step away from him, but the ground was uneven, and she stumbled. 'Please.'

Her voice was a whisper.

'Do what?' His head came closer to hers, close enough to feel the whisper of his breath on her lips.

Angie kept her eyes on Liam's as his head dipped closer. She held her breath and watched as a muscle jumped in his jaw. For all his words, he was as skittish as she was. She lifted her chin a notch, about to challenge him, when his lips swooped onto hers. She should have struggled, but instead, she reached up and gripped his arms. Her lips opened to welcome a kiss that was a mix of desire and anger, and she returned it as though it had only been hours rather than long months since he had last held her in his arms.

Gradually, the anger receded, and his lips clung gently to hers as though he was reluctant to finish the moment and let her go. Angie held his arms firmly, this time pushing him away as she turned her head from his lips. His mouth slid gently across her cheek, and she sighed. The first time Liam kissed her, he feathered a kiss across her forehead and slid soft lips across her cheek until he teased the corner of her lips. She had never forgotten it. Two years later, the memory still gave her goosebumps.

He stepped back, and she dropped her head, letting her hair fall over her face.

'Why did you have to go and kiss me like that?'

Chapter Fourteen

Liam dropped the large food cooler on the side of the rug and stood staring at the sky. It had turned dark in the time it had taken to retrieve the coolers and walk back to the showground. Angie strode ahead of him, carrying the smaller cooler. She'd dropped it on the side of the rug, made a quick excuse to Lucy about having to see someone, and disappeared without another word.

'Is everything okay, Liam?' Lucy asked quietly. Garth was holding the baby, and she reached over and opened the lid of the cooler.

'Yes. All good.' His words were clipped, and he waved away the plate she offered him. 'I'm going over to the beer tent to grab a beer. What time do you think you'll be driving home?'

'After the eight o'clock fireworks, I think. Is that okay?' He must have been giving off some sort of vibe because Lucy was subdued and not in his face as she normally would have been.

'Yep. I'll make sure I'm back here before then. I'll help Garth load up when you're ready.' He nodded and strode off to the beer tent, conscious of the disappointment on Lucy's face.

Stupidest thing he'd ever done—well, up there with one of the most stupid—was coming to the show and then finishing it off by kissing Angie. When she'd held his arms and pulled back, regret had ripped through him. Not regret that he'd kissed her, but regret that she'd wanted him to stop. He stopped beside the ring where a rodeo was underway and gripped the timber rails. She had kissed him back, and for a brief moment, he'd thought—and hoped—that everything was going to be okay. That everything would go back to the way it had been.

But how could it? He was a fool. She was engaged. He closed his eyes, still able to feel the soft warmth of her lips beneath his. If he'd had his own car, he'd jump in, make sure the farm was secure, and drive to Sydney. As far from Prickle Farm, Prickle Creek, and Angie as he could get.

London would be good.

He'd done the wrong thing. She was with someone else now. He'd been foolish to tease her when he couldn't resist her response. Her eyes had said that she wanted him; otherwise, he wouldn't have kissed her. It had been a low act when she was engaged to another man, but for the love of God, he'd not been able to help himself. And to make it worse, he knew he'd do it again if she looked at him like that. The only solution was to get away. And that brought his thoughts around in full circle. He'd be going away again soon, and she'd be staying here, so there was no point in trying to start anything anyway.

There was no future for them. There was no point dreaming about one. She had whatever-his-name-was, a successful vet practice, and her own future stitched up.

And what did he have? A love for Angie that he'd never admitted to himself and had certainly never shown her. He'd let her slip through his fingers when she'd come back to Australia, kidding himself that his career was more important to him than she was.

He'd stuffed up big time, and now he had to let her get on with her life.

But he couldn't go anywhere yet; he had responsibilities here, at least until Sebastian came back. Gran and Pop were flying home for a while next week and were going to rejoin the cruise until they came home for Christmas. He couldn't leave until Sebastian was settled in.

Damn it, Sebastian was still in Europe, or he'd get him to

come back to Prickle Farm sooner.

And double damn, there was the blasted dog, too. What the hell was he going to do with Willow when he left? He'd made a right royal mess of his time here, and all it had taken was one simple kiss to show him that.

'Liam.'

He turned as his name was called. Jim Ison was leading a horse out of the enclosure.

'Jim.'

'I just have to rub down Molly, and I'll be over to have a beer. Have you got a spare half hour, and we can catch up?' Jim waited at the wide gate as Liam opened it for him.

'Yes. Perfect timing. I was just heading over there myself.'

'Good. I'll see you in ten minutes.'

Liam closed the gate behind Jim and the horse and headed along past the main ring, down the back of sideshow alley, and across to the open-air beer tent. Even though he wasn't really looking—he was kidding himself; his eyes were scouring every dark corner—there was no sign of Angie. Despite what she'd said about seeing someone, he was sure she went home. It was only a few hundred metres from the showground to the main road into town. Laughter and voices filled the air as he walked across to the bar. He bought two cans of beer and waited for Jim to join him.

At least talking about the alliance would take his mind off Angie.

Guilt tugged at him. He should call her later just to check she was okay.

He might call her just so he could hear her voice.

***

Angie pushed open the door of the surgery. She'd sent Lucy a text saying that she'd had to come back to town, implying that she had a patient without actually lying about it. She couldn't stay there a minute longer. Liam's kiss had set a fire in her belly and regret in her heart, and she didn't trust herself if she saw him again. She might be forced into his company, but she would move heaven and earth to ensure they were never alone. She trusted Liam. It was her emotions she couldn't trust. When he'd kissed her, she'd almost cried.

Poor Lucy. Angie hoped that she and Garth had enjoyed the picnic alone because she knew that Liam hadn't stayed with them either. On her way to the exit gate, she'd stepped behind one of the temporary buildings as she'd seen him striding along. He'd stopped at the ring and watched the horses for a while, and she'd taken the opportunity to slip away. It had only taken her half an hour to walk back into town. Luckily, she had her keys, purse, and phone in the pocket of her dress.

Her phone beeped as she headed out to the back. While she was here she might as well check on the two patients she had in the dog hospital. She opened her purse and pulled out her phone.

The text was from Lucy. **Hope U're ok. I know something happened, but Liam had a face like thunder. Coffee soon?**

Her fingers flew over the buttons as she texted back. **I'm okay see U soon.**

If Lucy hadn't sent them off to the car together, nothing would have happened. But Angie knew she was as much to blame as Liam. Damn it, she just couldn't resist him. She'd never been able to; not since the first minute she'd laid eyes on him. That lazy smile, the special look in his eyes when he gazed at her, and the full lips that enticed…

But this time, she had her eyes wide open. She was simply a convenience to him. She was here in Prickle Creek, and Liam was obviously going to make use of that until he took off again.

And he would go. Anger began to simmer in her chest. How

dare he? When he knew—or thought—she was engaged to another man. It didn't matter that she wasn't. For all intents and purposes, he thought she was.

***

'Mate, that's great. What you've discovered in less than a week is more than we would ever have imagined. Bloody, dishonest bastards. Not only are they pulling the wool over the eyes of everyone with their environmental statement—'minimal and manageable risk to the environment,' be damned—they've lied to their shareholders, too.' Jim was pleased with the information Liam had unearthed.

'So what's the next step?' Liam took a swig of his beer.

'We'll take it slow and easy. We'll keep consolidating our position, and gather more information. Most of the farmers have put locks on their main gates, so the pipe layers can't have access to their properties, and it's only a matter of time—'

Liam tuned out as Jim continued. The sky lit up, accompanied by a loud whoosh that was followed by a bang as the first skyrocket was launched. A myriad of red and white stars exploded and drifted to the ground in the middle of the main ring, accompanied by the oohs and aahs of the crowd.

'So, we'll meet the week after next and plan our next step.' Jim held his hand out and shook Liam's firmly. 'Thanks for all your work. Appreciate it.'

Liam finished his beer and put the empty bottle in the bin next to the door. As he made his way back to the picnic area, he kept an eye out for Angie, but there was no sign of her. Garth and Lucy were sitting on the rug, and James was asleep in his pram. The coolers and the picnic baskets were packed up.

'We're ready to go if you are.' Lucy's voice was subdued. 'No point staying for the second show; we've seen the fireworks, and James is sound asleep. He'll be due for a feed by the time we get home.'

Liam couldn't help himself. 'Where's Angie?'

'She had to go back to town.' Lucy stared at him, but he wasn't going to share what had happened.

'How did she get there?'

'I guess she walked.'

'Okay.' He reached down and lifted the cooler, and Garth picked up a couple of boxes and hefted one onto each shoulder.

'I'll wait here till you come back for the rest.' Lucy's voice was sad. 'No one had a very good time, did they?'

Guilt trickled through Liam, and he injected enthusiasm into his voice. 'I did. And I also had a chance to talk to Jim Ison. And look, you and Angie won your stuffed toys.' He nodded over at the pram. 'And young James looks like he had a great time. You've worn him out.'

'Thanks, Liam. But I don't believe you.' Lucy finally smiled. 'As long as Angie is okay. She looked really upset.'

'Leave that be, Lucy. I'm going to sort it.'

And he was. It was time for him and Angie to talk it out.

Whatever this thing was between them. He'd go into town this week. He smiled as he thought of the perfect excuse.

Willow was due for her second vaccination.

Chapter Fifteen

As it turned out, Liam didn't get to town in the first half of the week. The tractor broke down, two steers got stuck in the dam, and the water pipe in the bore took a whole day to fix. Each morning, he started out with great intentions, and Willow looked up expectantly as he ate breakfast at the kitchen sink. 'I'm sorry, pup. I've been ignoring you this week. We'll go to town and see Angie soon, I promise.'

Early on Wednesday afternoon, he came in and had a quick shower, planning to head to town to catch her before she closed the surgery for the afternoon. He didn't call to make an appointment. He'd take a chance on showing up. Knowing Angie, if she knew he was coming in, she'd disappear like she had the time he'd gone to pick Willow up. As he'd dealt with recalcitrant cattle, uncooperative motors, and twisted pipes this week, he'd practised what he would say to her.

After Willow had her shots and Angie had finished her appointments for the day, he would take her to the milk bar, and they would have a civilised chat. He picked up Willow's lead. The pup could sit outside the milk bar while they chatted—like the two mature adults who knew each other well and who were going to be friends until he moved away. Liam nodded. He had it all planned. Emotions had been put aside. As he picked up his keys, a vehicle rattled across the cattle grate, and he crossed to the window. He wasn't expecting anyone, and the front gate was padlocked. He leaned forward with a frown, and then a smile spread across his face as the car door opened.

***

Angie closed the surgery early on Wednesday afternoon.

Cissy had to go to Narrabri to the dentist—that was another service that Prickle Creek had lost as the town got smaller—and there had been no appointments scheduled after three o'clock. She picked up the hard drive with the month's financial records on it and headed home. She'd put off doing the accounts for too long, and it was the perfect opportunity to catch up on her accounting.

After a short walk home in the late spring sunshine, she pushed open the door to her small house and put the hard drive on the desk next to her personal laptop. Spreadsheets and numbers were her pet hate. She couldn't think of anything she disliked more. She closed her eyes. Yes, she could, but she wasn't going to go there. She had managed to put Liam nicely into a space in her head where she didn't have to think about him. Occasionally, he would pop into her thoughts like a nagging toothache, but she firmly pushed the thought—or image—away and moved on to something else. Consequently, she had kept herself very busy since she had left the show.

The surgery was spotless—Cissy had looked at her as she had scrubbed out cages and cleaned out cupboards—her house was clean, the cupboards and drawers were in perfect order, the washing and ironing were up to date, and the pantry was well stocked. Although when she had slipped into the supermarket to shop, she'd kept an eagle eye out for any sign of Liam, but sadly—only because it showed how badly the town businesses were suffering—she had been the only one in the store, along with the cashier.

It showed how desperate she was to keep her mind occupied that the hard drive was now sitting there looking at her, waiting for her to start work. Angie procrastinated, taking a long shower and washing her hair. Then she sat at the kitchen table and painted her fingernails and toenails as the hard drive stared back at her.

The house was quiet and empty. For the first few months

back in Melbourne from London, she'd kept herself busy working as a locum across the city, and by the time she'd driven back to her small flat there each night, it had been time for dinner, and then she'd crash into bed, exhausted—from her work and her emotions.

It had taken a long time before she'd regained control. It would be good to get to know some of the young people in this town.

After Liam left. She wasn't going to risk going out while he was still around. Sally had called about a meeting for the Bachelor and Spinster ball this morning, and Angie had promised to attend the meeting at the RSL on Monday night.

But now she was bored.

Angie walked into the living room with her computer beneath her arm and flicked the television on. Maybe some background noise would make the idea of doing accounts more attractive. Her gaze settled on the small Christmas tree next to her chair, and loneliness stung afresh. Cissy had decorated the surgery for Christmas yesterday, and it had inspired Angie to go and buy the small tree from the two-dollar section at the back of the grocery store.

Stupid, really, when I'm the only one who will see it.

She went back to the kitchen and put the jug on to boil. When she'd made her coffee, she fired up the computer. She couldn't put it off any longer. As she was about to launch her business program, her phone rang from the kitchen benchtop.

She glanced at the number and pressed answer. 'Hi, Lucy.'

'Angie! How are you? I tried to call the surgery, but there was no answer. Are you okay? You're not sick, are you?'

Angie laughed. 'No. I'm playing hooky. Cissy had to go to Narrabri, and I decided to take an early mark. It's a bit of a worry, actually. It's been really quiet this week.'

'Don't worry. Enjoy the time to yourself. It's always quiet

in town after everyone recovers from show weekend.' There was a pause, and Angie waited as Lucy's voice softened. 'I rang to make sure you weren't cross with me?'

'Why would I be cross with you?' Angie crossed to the window and looked out as a car screeched down the street, its tyres screaming on the bitumen as it came to a sudden stop, and a group of schoolchildren stepped off the curb. 'Silly idiot!' she muttered under her breath.

'I know I was, and I'm sorry.' Lucy's voice was contrite.

'Don't be silly. I was talking about the idiot who almost ran down some kids from the primary school.' Angie laughed as she reassured Lucy. 'And what do you have to be sorry for?'

'Last Friday. Trying to push you and Liam together at the show. I know it didn't turn out well. You took off, and he looked really upset.'

'Did he?' Angie said slowly.

'He did. I won't ask what happened. Garth got stuck into me when we got home and told me to mind my own business. He said if you two are meant to be together, it'll happen and I don't have to help it along. I promise I'll pull my head in.'

'It's all okay, don't stress yourself. I've had such a busy week I've barely given Liam a thought.'

'Really?'

'Really.'

'Oh, that's fabulous. I so didn't want to hurt our friendship.'

'Don't worry. Everything is good. We're fine, you and I.'

'Now that I know that, I was hoping you'd come out and have dinner with us tonight. As long as you don't mind driving all the way out from town.'

Angie pursed her lips and frowned. 'Us? Don't think I don't trust you, but who else will be there?'

'It's okay. I'd be the same if it was me. It's just me and

James. Garth is at a meeting in Coonamble. I could do with the company. Some girl time!'

Angie nodded. 'Sounds good to me. Girl time is just what I need. What can I bring?'

'Nothing. I don't need anything and you can talk to me while I cook. Do you like pizza?'

'I do. I'll bring a bottle of wine.'

'Oh, Angie, I'm so pleased you said yes. Why don't you come out now before it gets dark.'

'I will.'

Angie looked triumphantly at the hard drive sitting on the desk. 'I guess you'll have to wait.'

***

Liam ran down the back stairs, followed by Willow, as the door slammed on the unfamiliar car. 'What are you pair doing at home? We didn't expect you till next week?' He reached out and hugged his grandmother and then shook Pop's hand before he turned back to Gran.

'Look at you!'

Gran wore a stylish dress, and her hair fell softly around her face. A matching handbag and smart shoes completed the outfit. A soft pink flush ran up her cheeks and Pop smiled.

'Pretty swish, isn't she? I took her shopping and we've filled a suitcase with a new wardrobe.'

'Get away with the pair of you.' Gran flapped her hand and then pointed at the car. 'It wasn't the only shopping we did. Do you like Harry's new car?'

'I do. Liam whistled and walked around the luxury sedan. 'I'm surprised you brought that out on the dirt roads.'

'It'll clean.' Pop walked around to the back of the car with Liam to unload the boot, as Gran bent down to pat Willow. 'What's with the padlock on the front gate?' he asked. 'Been having some trouble?'

'No, just a precaution. I'll tell you all about it over a cup of tea.'

'Just as well Harry had a key to open it.' Gran looked at him. 'You're in early from the paddocks. Were you heading out?'

'I was just going to take Willow into town for her needles.' Liam wasn't sure whose eyebrows rose the highest. He managed to keep the disappointment from his voice. It looked like he wasn't meant to catch up with Angie today.

'Willow?' Pop's mouth opened in a wide grin. 'What breed of working dog is she?'

'Another story to tell you over a cup of tea.'

Liam reached over and hugged Gran again. 'Honestly, Gran, you look amazing. The months away have done you a world of good.'

'And she's learned how to shop. I had trouble keeping her away from the stores. There's a whole suitcase full of baby clothes there.' Pop put his arm around Gran.

'After we have a cuppa and get changed, we'll go over to the Mackenzies and see our first great-grandson.' Gran's smile was wide. 'I can't wait to see him. Don't call Lucy. I want to surprise her.'

Liam headed for the kitchen to put the kettle on.

Chapter Sixteen

Angie snuggled James against her shoulder and buried her face in his soft, downy hair as she watched Lucy roll out the pizza dough. He smelled of baby powder and sweet milk, and a pang of longing shot through her.

One day. When her surgery was up and running and she had paid off her loans. And when she met someone she wanted to share her life with. Someone who would stay with her. Maybe there was someone out there for her.

'There's nothing like the smell of a clean baby, is there?' Lucy reached over and popped a kiss on James' head on her way to the fridge. 'Never thought I'd be married and a mum by twenty-five.'

'So we're the same age. I was twenty-five in June,' Angie said.

'You're doing well to have your own business.' Lucy chopped the basil she'd got from the fridge, and the pungent aroma surrounded them.

'My mum left me some money when she died. My grandparents' house was sold as a part of the estate, and it gave me a good deposit for the business once the rest of the debts had been cleared. Although I still have a pretty hefty business loan.'

'Where's the rest of your family?' Lucy wiped a hand over her face and Angie smiled as a white streak of flour coated her forehead. She shook her head.

'I don't have any. Just me.' She looked up at Lucy. 'I have a father somewhere but he didn't want any contact with me after he left Mum.'

'Oh, sweetie. That's so sad.'

'I'm used to it. He has another wife and a couple of kids now but he wanted to cut all ties. I didn't even call him to let him know Mum died.'

'Oh, Angie.' Lucy—bless her—had tears in her eyes.

'It's okay. I've gotten used to being on my own. It made it easier to understand and cope when Liam let me go without a fight. I'm used to it.' She shrugged. 'I've got the knack with animals, but I guess my upbringing stuffed my chances with relationships. Just a bit unlovable.'

Lucy stood there, mouth open, hands on hips. 'Don't you dare say that! You are the loveliest person. Don't you ever think that Liam would have thought that, either? He was always a bit selfish, but he's grown up over the past few months. Since he's been home on the farm.'

'Liam kissed me the other night. At the show.' Angie spoke quietly. It was time to spill to Lucy. Girl talk was girl talk, and she knew she could trust Lucy. It wouldn't go any further.

'And?'

'Oh, Lucy.' Angie put her free hand to her eyes. 'It was wonderful. It was as though the year and a half we've been apart just disappeared.'

Lucy walked across to the sink and washed her hands, her back to Angie. For a while she didn't say anything. 'So what are you pair going to do about it? You both obviously still have feelings for each other.'

'That may be so, but it won't work. I'm here to stay, and Liam will go back to the city. He will.'

Lucy shook her head. 'Maybe not.'

Angie didn't say what she was thinking, but the thought stayed in her head. Even if they both did stay here, Liam would lose interest in her. She knew it but didn't want to upset Lucy by saying it again. After all, he was Lucy's cousin, and she would stick up for him.

'So, what sort of pizza are we having?'

Lucy looked at Angie, her gaze narrowed. She nodded, obviously accepting that the topic was now closed. Fifteen minutes later, the aroma of baking pizza filled the kitchen, and Angie opened the bottle of red wine while Lucy fed and changed James.

She picked up her glass and wandered into the living room. One wall was covered with family photos, and she smiled. Some of the photos were outstanding; Lucy had mentioned that Sebastian, one of the other cousins, was a world-class photographer. The four cousins were all good-looking adults. And she'd heard that Jemima was a model in New York. Good family genes there.

She put her wine glass on a coaster on the coffee table, leaned forward and looked at a photo of Liam sitting on a bale of hay. He was staring past the camera and his expression was sombre. A tingle started at her toes and worked its way up to her lower belly.

Damn it all. What chance did she have when just a photo of Liam could get her warm and tingly?

'Oh my God.' Lucy's high-pitched squeal reached her, and Angie grabbed her glass and hurried back into the kitchen.

'What's wrong? Did you cut yourself? Is James okay? What happened?' Angie put her glass on the countertop and hurried across to Lucy, who was standing looking through the kitchen window. She turned to face Angie, her eyes sparkling and her face wreathed in a huge smile.

'Gran and Pop are home! I had no idea they were coming back!'

Angie stepped back as Lucy headed for the door and pushed it open. She disappeared down the steps, her ponytail swinging behind her. Angie took a deep breath, folded her arms, and leaned back on the bench, looking out of the window. Not only were the grandparents here to visit, but Liam was holding the gate open for them. Angie's heart thudded, and she swallowed, trying to grab the tendrils of panic that were winding themselves around her heart. As soon as she was introduced, she'd say her goodbyes and leave the family to catch up. It wasn't the place for her to be. It was intrusive. She tipped her wine down the sink, rinsed her glass, and put it in the drainer, surprised to see her hand shaking. It would be the first time she'd faced Liam since he'd kissed her.

And I kissed him back.

She stood at the window and watched as Lucy hugged the older couple one at a time. Liam was still by the gate and staring at the window. It was too late to step back out of sight, so she lifted her hand in acknowledgement. Whether Lucy had told him she was in there or whether he had sensed her…

God, don't be stupid. Her car was parked by the shed, and he would have seen that. Of course, he knew she was in here. Taking a deep breath, she crossed the kitchen, picking up her handbag on the way. She pushed open the screen door and stood to the side of the veranda as the chatter washed around her.

'Oh, Gran, wait till you see James. He is so big and the most beautiful boy in the world.'

'And your grandmother wore a hula skirt in a concert on the cruise ship.'

'I have a whole suitcase of presents in the car. Liam, get them out for me, please.'

Angie wiped her hands down the sides of her jeans. They were damp with perspiration as her nerves kicked in. She just wanted to get in her car and make a hasty exit back to town.

Lucy and Liam noticed her at the same time. Liam smiled and butterflies took up residence in her stomach instantly. Lucy frowned.

'Angie, put your bag away right now. You're not going anywhere!' Lucy linked her arm through her grandmother's and walked up the steps with her, smiling at Angie. Sympathy underpinned the smile on her face. It was almost as though Lucy was trying to tell her, 'You can do it.'

'Gran, this is my friend, Angie. She's come out to have dinner with me. Angie, this is my gran, Helena.'

Helena smiled at her and reached for her hand. Her skin was soft, and her nails were manicured and painted a soft shell pink. 'Hello, Angie, it's lovely to meet you.' Her voice was cultured and held a trace of an English accent. Angie smiled back at the graceful woman.

'I'm pleased to meet you, too, Helena.'

Liam came over to the steps, carrying a suitcase in each hand. 'And this is Pop—Harry to his friends.'

Harry smiled and shook her hand, and Lucy giggled.

'Have you pair decided to move in with Garth and me?' she asked.

Her grandmother laughed. 'No, the suitcases are full of presents. Don't worry, they're not all for James. There are some for you and Garth, too.'

Angie felt more like a third wheel with each passing moment. She leaned over to Lucy. 'I'll head back to town now, Lucy. We'll catch up another time.'

Lucy took her by the shoulders and steered her towards the screen door. 'Oh, no, you don't, my dear girl. You're not going anywhere. I need someone to watch the pizza while I show off my lovely boy and open all my presents.'

Angie shook her head and knew that her face was getting pinker by the minute as Liam and Harry followed the three women into the kitchen. She was stuck here. In a room with Liam and half of his family. 'I feel like I'm intruding. This is a family night. I'll come back another night.'

It was Liam who insisted she stay this time. His deep voice was full of warmth. 'No way, Angie. We'd feel really bad if you left because we'd arrived. Besides, that pizza smells good, and knowing Lucy, she will be more interested in her presents than feeding me.'

'There's another one in the freezer, Angie. Can you pop it in the oven while I go and get James?'

Angie nodded and headed to the kitchen as Liam and his grandparents walked into the living room with the suitcases.

Freezer? All that was in the kitchen was a double-door fridge with an ice maker in the door. She looked across the room and spied a door leading to the veranda. She poked her head through the doorway. It was a large utility room with two chest freezers and boxes of vegetables on the floor. Lucy's call followed her out. 'Freezer on the left, bottom left basket.'

Angie lifted the lid and leaned in. There were three frozen pizzas in the basket. The boxes were as wide as the basket, and they were hard to get out. She leaned in and muttered as she tried to remove the jammed corner of the box from the basket, holding the freezer door open above her head with the other hand.

Suddenly, she was aware of warmth at the backs of her legs as someone stood behind her, and a large hand held the freezer door open for her.

Without looking, she knew it was Liam. 'Thank you,' she murmured as she used both hands to free the pizza boxes. She lifted two out and finally lifted her gaze to meet his as he let the door go, and it shut with a loud thud. 'Supreme or Ham and Pineapple?' she asked softly.

His green eyes were full of mirth. 'What do you think, Ange?'

'I think both because your grandfather looks like he would

have a hearty appetite.' She grabbed both of the boxes and went to move past him back to the kitchen, but Liam grabbed her on the way past, putting his arm around her waist.

'I was on my way to town to see you when the olds arrived.'

'Oh?' she said, lifting her brows in a question.

'Willow is due for her shots.'

'Oh.' *Wow, what scintillating conversation.* She stepped back, away from Liam's reach.

Disappointment flared briefly in his eyes and he lowered his voice. 'And I want to talk to you about the other night.'

'There's nothing to talk about, Liam. Forget it ever happened.' She lifted her chin and stared at him. 'I have. Now, please excuse me. I have pizzas to put in the oven. And then I'm going back to town. And don't try to talk me out of it.'

She flounced past him and went back to the kitchen, keeping herself busy as she took the first pizza from the oven and put it on the cooling rack by the sink. She took the other two from the boxes and put them on the countertop. She needed to find some more oven trays.

The afternoon light had faded, and she flicked the kitchen light on, surprised to see that he was still in the kitchen with her.

'I can do this. You go in with your family,' she said.

'No. I'll help you, and then we can both go into the living room. I'm giving Lucy some time with Gran and Pop. They were so disappointed that they were overseas when James arrived early. They've cut their cruise short to come and see him.'

'Are they home to stay?' Angie tried to hide the real curiosity in her voice. If they were staying Liam might leave sooner.

He obviously picked up the intent of her question. 'No, they're only here for a few days, and they're flying to Perth to rejoin the cruise ship.'

'Oh.'

'But they'll be back for Christmas, and then they're going to England for a few months to catch up with Gran's relatives.' He took a step closer and Angie had nowhere to go. 'Are you sure you're okay, Ange?'

'Of course I am. Why does everyone keep asking that?'

'Because we all care about you. Lucy does, and of course I do, too.

'Huh. Do you?' she muttered under her breath as she ripped at the plastic cover of the pizza box, but it wouldn't tear. Looking around, she opened a drawer, pulled out a knife and slit the plastic. 'Do you know where Lucy keeps the oven trays?'

'No, I don't.'

'Would you go and ask her, please? I don't want to poke around in her cupboards.' Angie was proud of the control she was keeping. Having something to do kept her mind focused and held her burgeoning emotions at bay.

'Oh, look.' Lucy's squeal reached them and cut through the tension that was building. 'Oh, Gran, it's gorgeous. Angie, Liam, come and see what Gran and Pop brought home for James.'

Angie stepped past Liam and walked into the living room, but she was aware of him close behind her.

A stand with a mobile of multi-coloured fabric animals sat on the floor with a rainbow-coloured mat at the base. 'He will love that. He's already starting to take notice of things. Thank you so much, Gran . . . and Pop!'

Angie looked across at Helena; she was holding James and looking down at him with pure love on her face.

Angie's throat closed as she shifted her gaze from one family member to another. Liam was laughing at something that Harry had said, and Lucy had her arm around her grandmother's shoulders. The love in the room was obvious, and Angie had never felt more alone in her life. Her mother's parents had died before she was born, and her paternal grandparents had not been in touch since her father had left her and Mum. Now that Mum was gone, she had no one in her life.

Apart from an imaginary fiancé. How pathetic is that?

Angie fought for breath as a huge, lonely chasm seemed to open in her chest, and she had no idea how she managed to speak normally.

'It's beautiful. He's a very lucky little boy. To have so many people who love him.' Her voice was bright and strong, and she amazed herself with the even tones she managed to get out. 'Now, Lucy, tell me where your oven trays are, and then I am going to leave you and your lovely family to catch up. I wasn't going to stay late because I have a heap of paperwork to do tonight.' Her words almost ran over each other, and she was pleased when Lucy didn't argue. 'We'll catch up another night, okay?'

'The trays are in the huge slide-out drawer under the stove,' Lucy said as she took James back from his great-grandmother. Angie noticed a look and a quick nod between Liam and Lucy as she turned back to the kitchen.

She crouched in front of the drawer and pulled out two oven trays, conscious of someone standing behind her. She couldn't— just couldn't—deal with Liam the way she was feeling. Her nerves were stretched tight like a rubber band about to snap, and one word from him would bring her undone. She pushed herself slowly to her feet and turned around, but it was Lucy's voice that reached her.

'Angie, I do understand why you want to leave. I'd rather you stayed, but I know how hard it is for you to be around Liam.'

Angie nodded mutely, not game to speak, or she would burst into tears.

'Leave those pizzas. I'll sort them in a while.' Lucy walked over and held her arms open. 'Give me a hug, girlfriend. I'll come into town in a day or two, and we can finish our natter.'

Angie hugged Lucy back, and this time, her voice shook. 'Thank you for understanding. Say goodbye to your grandparents for me. I'm sure I'll get to meet them when they come home again.' She picked up her bag, dug her keys out, and put her head down as she pushed open the kitchen door. She drove away without looking back and managed to keep the tears at bay until she was on the main road back to town.

Chapter Seventeen

Liam looked up as Lucy walked back into the living room. At the same time, he heard a vehicle cross the cattle grate and the dogs barking. 'Is that Garth home already?'

'No.' Lucy looked at him long and hard. 'Angie went back to town. She said she wanted to give us some family time.'

'Shit.' He ran his hand through his hair as Gran frowned at him.

'Watch your language in front of the baby,' she said.

Liam turned away and rolled his eyes at Lucy. 'Sorry, Gran. Sorry Lucy.'

'Come and help me with the pizza, Liam.' Lucy turned to Gran. 'Would you like to change James, Gran?'

Liam followed Lucy into the kitchen as Pop carried James into the nursery, Gran shooting them an interested look as they went up the hall. Lucy's mouth was set in a straight line, and she opened the oven to check the pizza and then closed it with so much force that the pans on the stove rattled.

'What's wrong?' Liam leaned back against the benchtop as she stared at him without a smile.

'Angie breaks my heart.'

Liam stared back at her, and his reply was terse. 'Why?'

'Because she's so bloody lonely.' Lucy opened the cupboard and pulled out some plates.

Liam took a breath. He didn't want to get into this conversation. 'She has a fiancé. It's not my fault that he never comes to see her.'

'No, nothing's ever your fault, Liam. You can't see what's right in front of you.' Lucy slammed the plates onto the table. 'Just like you couldn't see the truth when Angie left England.'

'She's been gossiping with you, has she?' Liam's voice rose slightly. He didn't like the idea of Angie baring her soul to Lucy, although he supposed he had to assume that her fiancé would know all about their previous relationship.

'No, she's found a friend to talk to, and as far as I can see, she doesn't have many in her life.' Lucy's voice softened, and she brushed a hand over her eyes. 'And are you aware she doesn't have any family at all? None. Just a father who doesn't want to know her. No wonder she's self-conscious around the family. I'm sure that's why she left in such a hurry. She couldn't bear to see us playing happy families.' Lucy's bottom lip trembled. 'Imagine how hard it will be for her when Jemmy and Seb are here, too. The whole crowd of us. I was going to ask her to spend Christmas Day with us, but I don't think that would be such a good idea.'

'Don't forget she has a fiancé to go to. Don't try to blame me, Lucy. Angie moved on very quickly. Like I told you last year, if she hadn't been engaged when I came back home, I would have contacted her straight away.'

The look that she shot him was strange, and Liam frowned. 'What?'

'Nothing. But I think you pair need to talk and clear the air so everyone will be happy.'

'Come on, let's go back into the living room. Gran and Pop will wonder what's wrong, and I don't want to worry them about anything. They deserve this fabulous time they're having.'

Garth arrived home, and they sat in the living room sharing the pizza, watching James coo at the mobile as he lay on the rainbow mat. Liam couldn't settle as he worried about Angie being upset. Finally, he turned to Garth. 'Mate, can I borrow your ute? Pop can take his new car back home in a while, but I just remembered I need something in town.'

'Not a problem. I don't need it until morning. Drop it back when you get home, and I'll run you back to your place.' Garth reached into his pocket and threw the keys to Liam.

Lucy smiled and reached out to squeeze his hand as he walked past her. 'Good luck,' she whispered.

Liam stared at the road intently as he drove into town. It was the time of night when roos would appear out of the darkness and slam into the side of the car, and he didn't want to damage Garth's ute, so he flicked the headlights onto high beam and took the road a little slower than he normally would have. All the way to town, Liam's thoughts scurried back and forth. He thought of the months he and Angie had lived together in London and how happy she had seemed. She'd made their small flat cosy with her touch. He'd loved coming in after work to the warm and welcoming home she'd created, but he'd soon realised when she left that it had nothing to do with the bright prints on the wall and the small lamps that gave the room a romantic glow when they were snuggled together on the old sofa at night.

Once Angie had gone, the flat had the same décor, but it was cold and empty. She wasn't there. He'd missed her soft voice, her sweet laugh, and the press of her body against his at night. He'd missed everything that made up the beautiful package that was Angie. But he knew she was building her career in Australia, and he didn't want to take her mind off that.

But bloody someone had, he thought bitterly. Grant.

If she'd wanted him to come home with her, she would have asked him to come with her. To get over her absence, he'd spent most nights at the pub or taking assignments in other towns and had spent a lot of time on the road. If Gran hadn't called when she had, he probably would still be in London, caught up in his unhappiness.

He'd missed Angie, and when she'd told him she had a new

man and was going to marry him, he'd vowed to get over her and immerse himself in his career. Like he'd told Lucy, it had been too late to get in touch with Angie when he'd finally come home.

Now look at him, a cattle and wheat farmer in the outback of New South Wales, and he was content. Not entirely happy—he needed Angie in his life for that—but much more content than when he'd been working as a journalist.

What chance did he have of winning her back? He was going to try his bloody best to do it. Red dusty roads and gum trees lit up by oncoming vehicles flashed past, and Liam focused his attention back on the road ahead. It seemed to take forever to get into town, but finally, he turned into Main Street, drove past the vet surgery, and pulled up in the dark driveway beside the little house. He let out a sigh of relief when he spotted Angie's car in the open carport in the backyard. The lights were on at the back of the house, and he climbed slowly out of the car, still not sure what he was going to say to her. He knew why he was here but had no idea how to approach it. He'd take it slow and let Angie's reaction guide how much he said. That was the logical way to approach it.

But whichever way it went, he was going to be honest. His biggest fear was that even if he was honest, Angie wouldn't want him. She did have a fiancé, after all. But he owed her an explanation.

It was way past time for honesty.

What happened after that was an unknown.

***

Angie hurried into the bathroom and stared, horrified, at her reflection as Liam knocked on the door. She turned the cold tap on and quickly rinsed her face, but it made no difference to her swollen eyes and her red nose. Why was he here? And worse still, if she opened the door, he was going to see her looking like this. He'd want to know what was wrong, and there was no way she was going to tell him it was because she couldn't stand the thought of not having him in her life. When the car had pulled up in the driveway, she'd stopped at the side of the living room window, and her heart had just about stopped beating as Liam had climbed out of Garth's ute.

He knew she was home because her car was there and the lights were on. Maybe she could sneak out the back door and take refuge in the surgery? Maybe she could just be quiet and pretend she wasn't here.

She grabbed a towel and patted her face dry as he knocked at the front door. She took a shuddering breath and waited, hoping, praying he might think she was asleep, and he'd go away.

She was in no state to talk to Liam the way she was feeling. All the way home, she'd tried to convince herself that there was no future in loving him, but it hadn't worked. She was going to have to sell the practice and move away. Because even if Liam did move back to the city, he'd still come home to visit. His family was here.

All of the people he loved. And what a wonderful family he had. The love for each other was obvious. He was so very lucky. It was her dream to create a family like that, and it was time to pull up her big girl panties, stop feeling sorry for herself, and get on with her life. Enough of this wallowing in self-pity.

The knocking on the door got louder.

'Angie, are you awake? I need to talk to you.'

With a sigh, she plodded to the front door. She pushed her hair behind her ears with one hand while she flicked the lock with the other.

It was dark, and if she didn't turn the light on, Liam wouldn't be able to see her red-rimmed eyes.

'Liam? What are you doing in town?' Her voice sounded thick and husky to her own ears.

'I wanted to talk to you.'

'And you came all the way into town?' She peered at him in the darkness but couldn't see his expression.

'Can I come in?' Liam leaned forward as she held the door half open. 'Please, Angie? It's really important.'

Reluctantly, she pulled the door open, and he stepped inside to stand beside her on the small interior porch. She tilted her chin and finally met his green-eyed gaze. His eyes widened as he took in her face, and a frown wrinkled his brow.

'Jesus, Ange. Have you been crying?' He lifted his hand, and ever so gently, his thumb ran across the top of her cheek beneath her eye. That one simple gesture was her undoing. More tears sprang to his eyes as his gentle voice washed over her. 'Come here.' He held out his arms and there was no way Angie would resist stepping into the comfort of him.

Her head nestled on his shoulder, and his large hand cupped the back of her head, holding her close. For a few long minutes, they stood like that, Angie taking comfort in the feel of Liam's hard chest beneath her cheek. Her tears dried up, and she closed her eyes, inhaling the fresh fragrance of his skin.

'Thanks. And don't worry, I'm okay. Just a silly meltdown. Stupid what struggling with spreadsheets can do to a girl's peace of mind. I never was any good with figures.' She tried to make light of it as she raised a shaking hand to her hair. 'God, I must look a mess.'

'You look beautiful. You always do. I guess I never told you that enough.' His voice was low and sent a ripple running down her spine.

Angie jerked her head up. 'Come inside.' She flicked the lamp on as she walked across the living room and gestured to a single chair, but Liam followed her over to the double sofa and took a seat beside her when she sat down. She moved to the far end and tucked her legs up beneath her, and looked at him warily. 'So, why the rush trip to town?'

'I could see you were upset when you left Lucy's, and I was right, wasn't I?' Liam moved a bit closer and picked up her hand.

Great, there went her excuse of spreadsheet depression. He could always read her feelings, except for the one time it had mattered.

He squeezed her hand gently, and Angie stiffened. Being so close to Liam was wonderful yet painful at the same time. Being with him just made her realise how hard it was not to be with him all the time. Those months together, in the same flat, sharing a bed and sharing their lives, had been taken for granted. It was only when you lost what you had, that you appreciated it.

And then it was too late.

Angie couldn't help watching Liam's thumb as it ran in small circles across the back of her hand. If she looked down, she could avoid looking at the muscles outlined by his tight white T-shirt. As he moved his thumb, his biceps strained and flexed.

God help me. She had to fight the rush of desire that ran through her.

He looked down, and she sensed he was choosing his words carefully.

'I want us to talk, Ange. I want you to know how much I regret letting you leave by yourself.'

'Don't, Liam. What's past is past.' Angie dug deep for a smile, pulled her hand out of his and folded hers together on her lap. If he wasn't touching her, it was easy to put on a front. 'And really, I'm fine.'

'Are you really?'

'Yep. I am.'

'You kissed me back at the show.'

'Old habits die hard.'

'Is that all it was?'

She nodded mutely as he moved closer to her on the sofa.

'What if I kissed you again now? What if I showed you I was going to fight for you? Would it be habit or something else?' He was so close she could smell his minty breath and feel the warmth of his skin almost touching hers.

Angie tried to scramble back along the sofa as panic and desire curled together in her stomach. 'Fight for me?'

'I should never have let you leave. I miss you.'

Her back was pressed against the back of the sofa, and Liam was edging closer with every word. Angie closed her eyes. She needed to feel his mouth on hers. She needed to have Liam touch her and to—

A soft gasp escaped her as he feathered a kiss on her forehead, and his lips lowered to slide against her cheek towards her lips.

'Now you're playing dirty.' She reached out and pulled him against her, hot skin against skin, lips against lips, and their breath mingling as he gently probed her mouth with his tongue. His body was hard and strong, so much tougher than when they'd lived together. Angie thought she'd die from the need to touch him. She ran her hands around his back, around taut muscles, and then down his toned, strong arms.

One last time. And she would live on the memory for the rest of her life. Her fingers crept to the bottom of his T-shirt, and she tugged it.

Liam stepped back and shook his head, tension in every line of his body. 'I'm sorry, Ange. I shouldn't have. It's not right with you being engaged. I'm sorry I overstepped the line, but damn it, it's so bloody hard.'

Angie swallowed before reaching out and taking his hand. He was entitled to the truth. 'Liam, I'm not engaged.'

She watched as his eyes widened, and a smile tilted that beautiful mouth. Of their own volition, her fingers crept down his chest and she pulled his T-shirt up, revealing a glorious expanse of muscled chest. As Liam's fingers held the bottom of her T-shirt, she leaned back and he peeled it over her head. His fingers crept up as the shirt was discarded and he gently cupped her bare breasts.

'I wasn't—'

Her intention to tell him she had never been engaged was cut off as his lips took hers.

'Oh, Ange. You are so lovely,' he murmured.

Chapter Seventeen

Angie woke slowly the next morning. She lay there for a moment, watching the dappled sunlight play on the wall beside the bed. In that moment between sleeping and waking, she wondered what the soft noise was, and as she turned her head, she smiled. Liam's head was beside hers on the pillow, and his forehead was almost touching hers. She moved her head slowly and softly across the white lace-edged pillowcase and rested her forehead against his. She couldn't believe he was here in her bed. The hours with Liam had been wonderful. No words, just like it had been when they were together before. Now, as she watched him sleep, Angie drank in the sight of him, imprinting him on her memory. His dark hair was messy and the dark stubble of his beard gave him a rakish look.

'Hello, my lovely.'

Angie jumped as his voice murmured beside her ear, followed by a gentle kiss.

'We need to talk.' His lips nuzzled her neck and she closed her eyes. 'I want to know more about what you said last night.'

'We do, but let's not waste time talking right now.' She ran her fingers down the side of his face. 'I have other things on my mind.' Angie didn't want to talk just yet. She wasn't ready to let him know that she loved him. Not yet.

'Wench,' he groaned. 'What time is it?'

She rolled over and picked up her phone. 'Almost seven.'

'Hell, I should have left by now. I have to get Garth's ute back to him.'

Her fingers crept down his chest and she heard the smile in his voice. 'But I guess it won't matter if I'm a little bit late.'

'Of course it won't. I'm sure he can talk to Lucy or play with James.'

Other matters interrupted any more conversation, and by

the time Liam ran for the shower in the small bathroom off Angie's bedroom, he was full of apologies.

'I've got a phone hook-up to Sydney for an interview this afternoon but I'll come back in tonight after you finish at the surgery. Okay?'

The joy that had filled Angie since last night died stone dead. She nodded and paused for a moment so that her disappointment didn't show. 'Okay.'

She managed a nod and waved at him, proud of how even she kept her voice 'I'll get you a clean towel. She climbed out of bed and ignored the crushing pressure on her chest, wrapping the sheet around her.

An interview. He was going back to Sydney just when she thought that maybe—just maybe—there was hope for them.

But she was wrong.

She wasn't going to do a temporary relationship.

When Liam left, that would be it. No matter what he wanted to say or promise her, she wouldn't listen. There was no future for them. He would love her and leave her. The lure of his career would take precedence over whatever he thought they could have between them. No matter what he was kidding himself into now.

Liam emerged from the shower, water dripping from his hair, and Angie handed him the towel, taking a last opportunity to run a loving hand over his chest.

She had no regrets. But she had a plan.

As Liam grabbed her and his lips took hers, his voice was intense. His words vibrated against her mouth. 'Ring me when you finish at the surgery this afternoon, and I'll come in and pick you up. We'll go out for dinner. You can tell me why you're not engaged anymore, and then we'll sort out what we are going to do.'

Angie's eyes burned with threatening tears, and she bit

down on the inside of her cheek until the pain was almost too much to bear, but she summoned up a smile. Her heart constricted painfully as the lie came from her lips.

'Tonight,' she said softly.

As he stood in the doorway and reached for her again, she grabbed the sheet above her breasts as it threatened to slip. With her spare hand she reached over and tucked in the tag on his crumpled T-shirt. Her eyes wandered over his face and body, drinking in the sight of him.

'Angie?' Liam put his hands on her shoulders and stared at her.

'Yes?'

'Okay?' His gaze burned into hers.

'Okay.'

Before Liam had even backed out of the driveway, Angie had her mobile out and was scrolling through her contacts.

***

'Angie, the delivery from Austin's is in the examination room; the first appointment is cranky, Mr Davis, and are you okay to go to the B&S Ball meeting tonight? Sally was on the phone to remind you as soon as I arrived.' Cissy rolled up the blinds on the front of the surgery. 'I said I'd pass the message on.'

'Um, no.' Angie jingled her keys nervously in her hand. 'I've had a bit of a family thing. I have to go to Melbourne.'

Cissy's eyebrows raised. 'Oh. When are you leaving?'

'I've got a locum organised, and I'll be leaving as soon as he arrives.'

'Today?' Cissy looked at her curiously and Angie nodded.

'I hope everything is okay.'

'Yep, nothing major.' Nothing apart from the fact that she was a coward. A coward unable to risk putting her trust in those little words that Liam had dropped as he left a couple of hours ago.

Angie had been on automatic pilot since then, ringing Steve, the locum who she knew was available for either short-term or long-term replacement. He'd just come off a long placement in Dubbo and was happy to help her out for as long as she needed. She just needed to find somewhere to stay in Melbourne where she was prepared to hide out until Liam moved on. And she needed to put some thought into whether she was brave enough to come back to Prickle Creek.

Yep. A coward.

##

'You are out in the sticks, here, Angie.' It was just after noon. Steve had arrived, and Angie gave him a quick tour of the surgery. 'But it looks like a great practice you've bought. Happy to come out and relieve you any time you need. My girlfriend has moved to Dubbo, so I'll take any Western work that comes up.'

'Thanks, I'll keep that in mind.' Angie and Steve had worked together on a few occasions and she knew he'd look after the business for her.

'You can bunk at my house. I've made up the bed for you in the bedroom off the kitchen. Help yourself to anything there.' Angie handed him the key. 'And Steve, thanks for being available at such short notice. I'll let you know when I'm coming back.'

'Like I said on the phone, I'm right till after Christmas.'

Angie saw Cissy's eyebrows rise.

'Are you driving right through to Melbourne today?' the vet nurse asked.

'No, Cis. I'm only going as far as Coonabarabran this afternoon.'

'Well, you drive safely then, sweetie.' She reached over and enfolded Angie in a motherly hug. 'I hope everything is okay.'

'Thanks, I'll give you a call when I get to Melbourne. And,' she held up her phone, 'I've always got my mobile on.'

ANGIE

Chapter Eighteen

'Come on, Willow. I've got a little surprise for you.' Liam grinned as he slipped the collar over the pup's neck for the second time. She was growing so quickly that he'd had to widen it by a couple of notches. 'We're going for a drive.'

He'd dropped Garth's ute back and Lucy's eyes had almost opened wide when he'd driven into the Mackenzie farm with the wheels spinning this morning.

'Sorry, I'm late, Garth. I got caught up in town.'

Lucy stood at the door waving them off, holding James, her smile wide, when they left for Garth to drop Liam back to Prickle Creek Farm. After an apology to Gran and Pop for staying out on their first night home, Liam changed into a fresh set of clothes and grabbed Willow's lead.

The farm work could wait. If he hadn't had to take Garth's ute back, he would have stayed in town with Angie. She'd been quiet when he left, and he wanted to get back there and sort things out. Liam wanted—no, he needed—to see Angie again. They should have talked this morning; he wanted to know when she had broken off her engagement.

And why.

Until he knew that, he wasn't going to assume anything.

But they'd not been able to keep their hands off each other, and the time for talk had disappeared in a haze of lazy loving.

Tonight he'd take her out, where nothing could distract them. Hell, it would have to be the RSL or the Chinese restaurant, not the most romantic setting, but they wouldn't get sidetracked if they were out in public. He was going to tell Angie Edmonds he loved her, and that he was never going to let her go again. If she wanted him, that was the sticking point.

He couldn't let her think too much. She'd always overthought things, and if he left her alone too long, she'd come up with some reason to avoid him. After last night, he wasn't going to let her go, but when he'd left, she'd been so quiet…

'I'll be back later this afternoon, Gran. I'll do some shopping in town and organise dinner.' He dropped a kiss on Gran's cheek as he headed out whistling. Pop patted Liam's shoulder as he went down the steps.

'Farm's looking great, Liam. You've done a grand job.'

'Thanks, Pop. I love it out here. I'll fill you in later, okay?'

'Take your time.' Pop winked at him. Lucy had obviously been talking.

As he drove past Angie's house, Liam noticed her car wasn't in the carport. Knowing his luck, she'd been called out to a farm visit. He parked the car and attached Willow's lead to her collar. Liam pushed open the door of the surgery and smiled as the pup plonked her butt on the step and refused to go in the door. He bent down and picked her up.

'It's okay, just a little jab, and I'm sure Angie will have a liver treat for you. If Angie's here,' he said, hopefully looking at Cissy as she came out of the examination room. The waiting room was empty, and Liam frowned as an unfamiliar man in a white coat followed Cissy. He held his hand out to Liam.

'Hi, I'm Steve Windell. I'm filling in for Angie. Who have we got here?'

'This is Willow.' Liam shook his hand and looked over at Cissy. 'Filling in?'

'Angie's gone to Melbourne. Some sort of family emergency.'

A chill ran through Liam. Bloody hell, he knew it. He'd frightened her off.

'When's she due back?'

'Not sure,' Cissy said. 'Maybe not till after Christmas.'

'What?' His voice came out in a croak as disbelief slammed through him. There was no family emergency. Angie had no family. It had to be something he'd said—or done. He tried to figure out what had happened. And what he had to do to fix it.

He wasn't going to let her go. No matter what she argued. No matter what she tried to use as an excuse. No matter where the former fiancé stood in the scheme of things. After spending the night with her, Liam knew they had a future. They were right together. He loved Angie, and he should have told her.

Hell, he should have told her months ago and not let her leave London. He'd known then that she was the most important thing in his life, but he'd been a coward.

Jobs didn't matter. Where they lived didn't matter.

Angie was all that mattered.

But he'd blown it again. He'd let her go again. Closing his eyes, he fought the cold despair that was settling in his chest.

Maybe it was too late. He shouldn't have left her this morning until they'd talked it out. Until he'd told her he loved her.

He looked up. Cissy and the locum vet were staring at him worriedly. He straightened as resolve flooded through him.

'Cissy, how long ago did she leave?' His voice was urgent.

'About an hour.' Cissy frowned, and then a smile crossed her face as she looked at him. 'But if you're thinking about following her, she's only going as far as Coonabarabran this afternoon.'

Steve scratched his head. 'She asked me about motels there and I told her to stay at the Cattlemen's Inn. They do a good feed there.'

Liam felt like kissing the pair of them. 'Can I ask a favour?'

Cissy nodded and held her arms open. 'You want to leave

Willow here?'

Liam passed the puppy over with a grin. 'I owe you one, Cissy.'

'It's fine. I'll take her home for the night. The kids will love her.'

Steve was shaking his head as Liam ran for the door. 'Thanks, guys.'

##

It was exactly one hundred kilometres from Prickle Creek to Coonabarabran. Liam glanced at his watch as he turned out of town onto the main road that led through the Warrumbungle Ranges. It was just after two o'clock, and he hoped that Angie hadn't decided it was too early to stop for the night. If she kept going, he'd have no chance of catching her up, and trying to find her in Melbourne would be impossible. He had to catch her; he had to tell her he loved her. A glimmer of what had gone wrong had come to him as he drove out of town. Angie had climbed straight out of bed when he'd mentioned that damned phone interview. She must have thought it was for a job interview in Sydney. Bloody hell, for a journalist, his communication skills were crap. He'd put off the call when he'd decided to come to town. The call to the journalist in Sydney who was working with him on the article for the Coal Seam Alliance could wait.

Not a bloody job interview. He slammed his hands on the steering wheel as the first road work stop sign appeared ahead.

God, please let her love me back. The words ran through his head in time with the wheels as the car ploughed on towards Coonabarabran. There was more traffic than he'd expected on the road, and the trip was slow. As he was held up by road works just past the Siding Spring Observatory turn-off, Liam came to a decision. If Angie would have him, he would stay on the farm and not go back to his career in journalism. Like Lucy said, there were plenty of social issues to deal with out here in the outback, and he could make a difference here. If Angie said no, he would deal with that, and he would accept that it was his fault. He'd blown it when he hadn't told her that he loved her in London. And he'd let her leave without him, putting his career ahead of her.

No more. Angie was the most important person in his life and he had to have faith. He knew she loved him.

By the time he hit the outskirts of Coonabarabran, Liam's stomach was in knots. It would serve him bloody well right if she was gone. It would serve him bloody well right if she was there and laughed because he'd followed her. It would serve him bloody well right if she didn't love him back. But whatever the outcome was, if it meant Angie's happiness, he would be satisfied with that. By the time Liam drove past the caravan park, across the Castlereagh River, and through the business district of the small town, his stomach was churning He glanced at the GPS on the dashboard; the motel was on the southern exit for town. His heart was in his throat as he spotted it ahead.

There was a high hedge at the front of the motel and along the drive leading to reception. The motel rooms and the cars were hidden from view. He pulled to a stop outside the office and climbed out of the car. A buzzer sounded as he opened the sliding glass door leading into the office. The desk was unattended, and he tapped his fingers on his thigh as he waited for someone to attend to him. Five slow minutes passed, and every scenario ran through Liam's thoughts as he waited. She hadn't stopped. She was there but would say she didn't love him. She'd say she loved him but wasn't prepared to take a risk on his staying around.

Jeez, where is the bloody receptionist? Every minute he waited added to the distance between Angie, as if she had decided not to stop. The problem was there were two different motorways you could take to go to Melbourne. He groaned and thumped his fist on his thigh as he turned for the door. As he opened it, a young woman in a navy skirt and white shirt stepped in.

'I'm so sorry to have kept you waiting. I'm on by myself and a guest who's just checked in, needed milk for her room.'

'Oh that's great.' He wondered if they would tell him if Angie was a guest or not. 'I was on the road behind my friend from Prickle Creek and I wondered if she'd arrived yet.'

The woman looked at him curiously as though sussing out what his intentions were. 'No, this is a single room.'

'Yes, that's fine. Could you tell me what room she's in?'

The receptionist shook her head. 'Sorry. No.'

There was only one way to get around it. 'Do you have another single for the night? For me?'

'One moment, please.' The woman walked behind the desk and clicked on the keyboard. 'Um, we're pretty full. There's a conference on at the RSL club. I only have one room left. It's the suite that we normally reserve for our wedding couples.'

'I'll take it.' Liam dug into his pocket for his wallet. Once he'd checked in he could look for Angie's car. He was going to look mighty foolish if it wasn't her who had checked in.

'Just the one night?'

'Yes, thank you.'

By the time Liam had paid, been given the key and had been directed to a parking spot at the far end of the motel, his heart was in his throat. He jumped in the ute, started it, and drove around the back of the reception area.

He closed his eyes briefly as joy surged through him.

Angie's car was parked at the far end of the building, next to the room he had just booked for the night.

'Thank you,' he mumbled.

Chapter Nineteen

Angie stood in the small kitchenette of the motel room, waiting for the kettle to boil. She opened one of those awful packets of instant coffee and tapped it into the mug before peeling back the foil on the long-life milk the receptionist had just dropped into her.

It had probably been silly to travel such a short distance for the first leg of her trip, but it didn't matter if she took a week to get to Melbourne. She had nowhere to go and no one to see when she got there. In fact, as she thought about it, there was no reason even to make Melbourne her destination; just because it had been home once and was familiar to her. There was no need to hide there and lick her wounds. She could go anywhere to fill in the time while she thought about what to do.

Angie poured the boiling water into the mug. She was unnaturally calm and determined not to feel sorry for herself. It was the right thing to do, to leave Prickle Creek. If she'd waited for Liam to come to see her tonight, she knew he would have asked her to stay with him until he went back to Sydney, and she wouldn't have been able to resist him. Just more heartbreak. Running away might have been the cowardly thing to do, but it was the easiest way to deal with it.

She sipped the hot coffee, ignoring the heavy feeling in her chest. She'd gotten over Liam before, and she'd do it again. If Steve was moving to the outback, maybe he was looking for a business to buy. She had no ties in the Pilliga and could start up another business anywhere else in Australia if needs be. It would mean losing the money she'd put into the business, but she could protect her heart. Once Liam had gone back to Sydney, she'd go back to Prickle Creek and put the practice on the market. Having Steve there for as long as she needed was a godsend. She hoped that business was good enough to pay him, and leave her enough to find somewhere cheap to live in the meantime.

She sipped at the coffee and wandered over to the window. The front of the room looked out over a colourful garden. Like Mum used to say when they were short of money: Something will happen, chicken. And it always had. They'd survived. Mum had even got her through university with that philosophy.

Angie opened the curtain and sighed. Something will happen.

She jerked back as a large figure walked past the window. Closing her eyes, she shook her head as the hot coffee sloshed out of her mug.

No. It couldn't be.

No. No. No.

Oh, jeez, something had happened, and it was the last thing she wanted. Or expected.

With a deep breath, she opened her eyes and stepped back from the window as someone knocked gently on the door. Okay, so something was about to happen.

Are you up there looking out for me, Mum?

Angie put the coffee mug down carefully. She looked down at the coffee stain on her pink T-shirt. That was the least of her worries. Walking over to the door, she hesitated before she lifted her hand to flick the lock open. There was no point in ignoring him, and she wanted to know how Liam had tracked her down.

The door opened slowly and there he was. All six foot plus of him, a hesitant smile gracing his face.

'Liam,' she said briskly, 'what are you doing here?' Her voice was steady, and her heartbeat had slowed to normal. He stood at the door, and Angie lifted her head to meet his gaze. Her stomach did a little dance as he looked back at her. His green eyes were full of…full of what?

Certainty? Tenderness?

'May I come in?' She was surprised to hear the tremor in his voice.

Angie stepped back and let him into the room. 'What are you doing here?' she repeated.

Liam closed the door gently behind him. He stood so close his fresh soapy fragrance surrounded her, and she could feel the heat of his skin. She dropped her gaze to the floor, not game to look at him. If she did, she was scared her heart would splinter into a thousand pieces.

Gentle fingers took her chin, and her heart began to thud.

'Look at me, Ange.'

She shook her head, and her lip trembled. Slowly he lifted her chin until she was looking into his beautiful green eyes. A little burst of hope radiated through her chest, and her heart stayed intact.

'I want you looking at me when I tell you something I should have said on a cold night in London last year.' His eyes were holding hers, and she couldn't have looked away if she had wanted to. 'Instead, here we are in a tacky motel room in the outback. Even if you don't want to hear this, even if it's too late, I want you to know.'

'Know what, Liam?'

'I love you.' His voice was tender as he ran his thumb gently along her cheek. 'I've loved you since I first saw you on a rooftop beer garden in London. And I'll love you for the rest of my life…if you'll have me.'

Angie closed her eyes as the first tear splashed onto her cheek. 'I—'

Liam shook his head. 'I'm so sorry it took me so long to

wake up. I've been a stupid fool.'

Angie lifted her hand to wrap her fingers around Liam's. 'But you're my stupid fool.' Another happy tear splashed down her cheek as Liam lowered his forehead to rest against hers.

'Oh, Ange. Do you really mean that? It's not too late?'

'It's never been too late, Liam. I've loved you since that same moment. On that rooftop at the Feathers pub.'

Liam's happy and relieved sigh warmed her cheek. 'Oh, sweetheart, say that again. No, let me say it again. Angie Edmonds, I love you.'

Angie leaned back and cupped his cheeks in her palms. 'Liam Smythe, I love you, too.'

His lips slid across her cheek towards her mouth, and a delicious shiver ran down Angie's back, but he paused before he reached her lips. 'I'm not kissing you yet. There's more to be said and sorted first. Let me finish. Listen to everything I have to say.' His warm finger touched her lips before she could finish. 'Really listen to me. This is something I should have asked you before I let you leave me in London.'

'What, Liam?'

He shook his head again and let go of her hand as he dug in his pocket. He pulled out his car keys and Angie frowned as he took one of the keys off the circle of steel that held it. As he watched, Liam put the keys back in his pocket, took her hand and pulled her to the door.

'Come with me.'

Angie was beyond words. She was still processing the three little words that Liam had said. *He loves me.*

Behind the car park, a high hedge blocked the motel from the road. A narrow strip of lawn in front of it held a tiny garden with rose bushes in bloom. Liam led her over to the small patch of grass, and still holding her hand, he dropped to his knee.

'Ange, I am not going to propose to you in a tacky motel room.'

'P-p-propose?' She looked down at him as he turned her hand over and kissed her palm gently and then wrapped his fingers around hers. She trembled as love for this man filled her.

'Angie Edmonds, will you do me the honour of being my wife?' Liam's voice was firm and strong, and he smiled as he held her gaze with his.

Tears splashed onto their joined hands as she looked down at their entwined fingers.

Lifting her eyes to his again, she nodded. 'Yes, Liam, I will marry you.'

He reached into his pocket again and smiled as he slipped the circle of steel from his key ring onto her ring finger. 'Just a temporary ring, but it makes it a formal engagement.'

He rose to his feet and slipped his arms around her. 'Now, before we say anything else, we are going to seal our promise with a kiss.' Angie needed no second bidding. She lifted her arms, linked her fingers behind his neck, and smiled as the ring flashed silver in the sunlight.

Her engagement ring.

##

It was almost half an hour before Angie and Liam went back to her room. He looked around. 'I guess it's not such a tacky room after all.' His smile was loving. 'Or is it that I'm looking at everything through rose-coloured glasses?'

'I think everything has a special glow this afternoon,' Angie said.

Liam pulled out the chair and pointed to it. 'I want you to sit down and listen to everything else I have to say. We should have everything clear between us.'

Angie sat. She reached out and took his hand. 'So, tell me.'

'You thought I was going back to Sydney? That I had a job interview?'

His expression stayed the same as she nodded. 'I did.'

'You were wrong.' Now a grin lifted his lips. 'Because I'm staying on the farm. I've already spoken to Pop about building my—our—house there.'

'You're not going back to Sydney?' Angie squeezed his fingers.

'No. Or London. Or anywhere else. Unless you want to go somewhere else, and then I'll follow you wherever you want to go.' His expression clouded into one of uncertainty. 'Now tell me about this Grant. I know you said you'd broken the engagement. But is that where you were going? To tell him that we were together? If you need to talk to him, I'll come to Melbourne with you.'

A laugh of pure joy bubbled up from Angie's chest to her lips. 'There's no need.'

'There is. I need to be sure that he knows we are engaged. No doubts, no uncertainties.'

Angie shook her head. 'We don't need to.'

'You've already told him?'

Angie smiled. 'Liam. I thought at one stage that Lucy must have told you. But she didn't break her promise, God love her.'

'Told me what?'

'There is no Grant. No Gary, no Geoff, no fiancé.'

His face was a picture for a moment as confusion was replaced by a huge grin. 'There's no ex-fiancé lurking in the wings? No one with a flash house in Melbourne near all the best coffee shops?'

Angie shook her head. 'He was only there so I could make a clean break from you.'

'Oh, sweetheart, that's something you don't have to worry

about.' Warm lips claimed hers, and happiness burst through Angie like the fireworks at the show. A few moments later, Liam lifted his head and there was laughter in his voice. 'There's only one thing we have to worry about now.'

Angie frowned. 'What's that?'

'Whether we are going to spend this afternoon and tonight in your room or whether we are going to move to my room. All the lovely lady in reception could give me was the bridal suite!'

'Just as well I haven't got my bag out of the car yet, isn't it?'

Liam's cheeky smile brought a giggle from Angie. 'It's just as well,' he repeated.

Chapter Twenty

Liam held Angie's hand tightly as they opened the gate at the edge of the driveway of Garth and Lucy's house. In his other hand, he carried a Santa sack full of gaily coloured presents, and Angie clutched Willow's new lead. The little pup had grown, and now she pulled, anxious to get to the house. The garden was a riot of colours and fragrant flowers. Angie smiled. It reminded her of Lucy's exuberance. Snapdragons, phlox, marigolds, and zinnias were clumped together haphazardly, but the effect was as soothing as Lucy's personality. The fragrance of summer roses filled the air, and the working dogs watched mournfully through the fence as Willow was allowed to walk across the soft green lawn to the house.

Lucy's smile had been like the cat that got the cream the morning that Liam and Angie had driven out to tell her they were a couple. When she related the story to Sebastian and Jemima after they arrived a couple of weeks ago, Lucy had taken full credit for them getting back together.

Angie's stomach twisted with excitement. It was the first time she'd been to a family Christmas party since she was a small child. Sitting with Liam on the floor of her living room—he and Willow had moved into town to Angie's house as soon as Sebastian had come home from Europe in the middle of December—wrapping presents over the past week had been fun, even with Willow getting tangled in the coloured twine.

'Angie! Liam! Where have you been? Everyone else is

here.' Lucy's excited voice reached them from the verandah as the smell of roast pork wafted around from the barbeque area that Garth had built, especially for the Christmas party. 'Gran won't let me open one present until everyone's here.'

Angie let go of Liam's hand and climbed the steps of the verandah.

'Merry Christmas, Lucy!' She hugged Lucy tight. 'And thanks so much for inviting me. You have no idea how special this day is to me.'

'Of course, you're here. You're one of the family now.' Lucy kissed Angie's cheek. 'Now, Angie, you come inside. Gran is holding court in the kitchen, and Jemima is pouring the wine. Liam, you put the presents under the tree and then go out and rescue Garth. Pop is telling him the best way to keep the new Weber hot. They're roasting enough meat to feed all of Prickle Creek.'

'Yes, ma'am!' Liam put his arm around Angie's waist and dropped a kiss on her lips. 'How crazy are we to have a roast dinner when it's going to be a stinker of a hot day?'

'It's an Aussie Christmas. And we've got plum pudding and custard, too,' Lucy protested.

'I'll be back in a minute. I have something for Angie, and I want the whole family to see it, too,' Liam said with a smile.

Angie frowned. 'See what?'

'Be patient, woman.' Liam dropped another kiss on her lips and headed inside with the presents.

'I wonder what he's up to now,' Angie said.

'It's Christmas Day, so I'm sure it's something special.' Lucy smiled.

'You know, don't you?' Angie nudged her as they walked towards the kitchen. 'I know that secret smile of yours, Lucy.' Angie detoured via the laundry and put Willow in the basket that was kept there for her.

'No chance, girlfriend. I kept your secret about Gary, the non-fiancé, so I'm keeping Liam's secret for him.' Lucy walked behind Angie into the kitchen.

'Grant!' Angie's giggle was loud.

'Yes?' Gran turned around wiping her hands on her apron.

Angie and Lucy laughed louder.

'Gawd, you pair, you're laughing like loons already and you haven't even had a Christmas wine yet.' Jemima walked over gracefully and hugged Angie. 'Merry Christmas, Angie.'

'Thanks, Jemmy.'

Angie gasped as she looked into the dining room adjacent to the kitchen. A long table was set with a white damask tablecloth, and silver cutlery shone beneath red candles that were already burning brightly. Red bon bons were at the side of each plate, and a crystal wine glass completed each setting.

'Oh. It's beautiful! I've never seen anything so lovely.' Angie clapped her hands with delight.

'It's a Christmas tradition,' said Gran, who had followed her to the door of the dining room. 'This is the first proper Christmas we've had out here for a long time, but Lucy insisted I bring over the family Christmas tablecloths and the special cutlery.'

The door from the verandah opened, and Liam came in, followed closely by Garth and Pop. James gurgled from the port-a-cot in the family room, the flickering lights of the Christmas tree keeping his attention.

'Present time.' Lucy jumped up and lifted James.

After Garth and Pop had greeted Angie, they all made their way to the family room. There was a quiet air of expectancy, and Angie wasn't surprised when Liam stayed standing in the centre of the room as the others all took a seat around the large room.

'What's going on?' she asked suspiciously.

Liam came over to her chair and stood in front of her. 'This is your first Christmas with our family, and I wanted to make it special and memorable for you,' he said.

'On your knee, Liam,' Lucy called out and the rest of the family smiled.

Heat ran up Angie's neck as Liam dropped to one knee and pulled a small silver box from his pocket.

'I know you've already got an engagement ring of sorts, and I know you thought we were going to Narrabri to see the jeweller next week.' Love shone from his eyes, and Angie blinked away the happy tears that threatened as he leaned close enough to whisper in her ear. 'I love you, Ange. More than life itself.'

He raised his voice and smiled at her. 'Now I really want you to feel a part of our family today and I could think of no better way than this.'

Angie smiled up at him and whispered, 'I love you, too, Liam.'

'Ange, will you do me the honour of accepting your real engagement ring, and let me tell you how much I love you in front of everyone that matters to me?'

Angie looked around at his family. The love in the room was there, and she knew it was for her, too. Even Pop wiped away a tear as he and Gran sat together on the sofa.

'Of course I will, Liam.'

Liam slipped the plain silver key ring circle—it had been on her finger since the afternoon in the motel—from her finger and put it on the table. He flipped open the small box, pulled out a ring, and slid it onto her finger. Sun shone through the window and Angie looked down at the brilliant light flashing from the sapphire and diamond ring until Liam's head moved closer to hers. Everyone apart from the man she loved disappeared from her view as Liam's lips clung to hers, and Angie closed her eyes.

She had a family. She had come home.

To Prickle Creek Farm. For Christmas.

For life.

Jemima's story is next.
Come and meet Ned.

Jemima:

eBook: *http://books2read.com/u/3GqOZa*

Print: *https://annieseatonstore.ecwid.com/Jemima-A-Prickle-Creek-Romance-PRE-ORDER-March-p712096834*

NOTE:
Previously published in the US as *His Outback Nanny.*

Also by Annie Seaton

Daughters of the Darling
From Across the Sea
Over the River
By the Billabong (2025)

A Bec Whitfield Mystery
Bowen River
Shadows on the Shore (June 2025)

Duckinwilla Days
Coming Home
Secrets and Surprises
Books 3-7 to follow in 2025

Home to the Outback *(2025)*
Lucy
Angie
Jemima
Isabella

Porter Sisters Series
Kakadu Sunset
Daintree
Diamond Sky
Hidden Valley
Larapinta
Kakadu Dawn

Others
Whitsunday Dawn

ANGIE
Undara
Osprey Reef
East of Alice
One Summer in Tuscany
Four Seasons Short and Sweet
Follow the Sun
Ten Days in Paradise
Deadly Secrets
Adventures in Time
Silver Valley Witch
The Emerald Necklace
A Clever Christmas
Christmas with the Boss
Her Christmas Star
The Emerald Necklace

The Augathella Girls Series
Outback Roads
Outback Sky
Outback Escape
Outback Wind
Outback Dawn
Outback Moonlight
Outback Dust
Outback Hope
Boxed Sets
Augathella Girls 1-4
Augathella Girls 5-8

Augathella Short and Sweet Series
An Augathella Surprise
An Augathella Baby
An Augathella Spring
An Augathella Christmas
An Augathella Wedding

ANGIE
An Augathella Easter
An Augathella Masquerade Ball
Boxed Set
Augathella Short and Sweet 1-3
Augathella Short and Sweet 4-7

Sunshine Coast Series
Waiting for Ana
The Trouble with Jack
Healing His Heart
Sunshine Coast **Boxed Set**

The Richards Brothers Series
The Trouble with Paradise
Marry in Haste
Outback Sunrise
Richards Brothers Boxed Set
Bondi Beach Love Series
Beach House
Beach Music
Beach Walk
Beach Dreams
The House on the Hill **Boxed Set**

Second Chance Bay Series
Her Outback Playboy
Her Outback Protector
Her Outback Haven
Her Outback Paradise
Boxed Set
The McDougalls of Second Chance Bay ***Boxed Set***

Love Across Time Series
Come Back to Me
Follow Me

ANGIE
Finding Home
The Threads that Bind
Boxed Set
Love Across Time 1-4

Bindarra Creek
Worth the Wait
Full Circle
Secrets of River Cottage
A Clever Christmas
A Place to Belong

About the Author

Annie lives in Australia, on the beautiful north coast of New South Wales. She sits in her writing chair and looks out over the tranquil Pacific Ocean.

She writes contemporary romance and outback crime and loves telling stories that always have a happily ever after. She lives with her very own hero of many years and they share their home with Barney, the rag doll puss, who hides when the four grandchildren come to visit.

Stay up to date with her latest releases at her website: **http://www.annieseaton.net**

If you would like to stay up to date with Annie's releases, subscribe to her newsletter here: **http://www.annieseaton.net**